SMIDGEONS

P.M. Kelly

Visit our website at
www.StillwaterPress.com
for more information.

First Stillwater River Publications Edition

ISBN: 978-1-958217-60-3

Library of Congress Control Number: 2022920627

1 2 3 4 5 6 7 8 9 10
Written by P.M. Kelly.
Cover illustration by Zach Card.
Interior book design by Matthew St. Jean.
Published by Stillwater River Publications,
Pawtucket, RI, USA.

*The views and opinions expressed
in this book are solely those of the author
and do not necessarily reflect the views
and opinions of the publisher.*

Dedicated to my brother Dikk,
A Larger than Life Character in a Small World

ONE

What a perfect night to watch shooting stars (if you believe in such a thing), and P.J. knew the best spot for this in the whole world was in his own back yard.

As he had a thousand times before, he lay flat on his back, on a pre-flattened, dew-drenched patch of green grass, staring so hard at each flickering dot that they seem to multiply the more he focused. P.J. had learned this technique from his father on a camping trip, back when they spent much more time together.

This evening was just for him. Tonight, he was a dedicated "telepathic explorer of the universe". All the while, he proceeded to devour his entire family-sized bag of sour cream-flavored potato chips, never once losing focus on the mission above him. This would be a night he will never forget. He just knew it.

P.J. marveled at how close the stars appeared to be. This cool, crisp night sky above was a blanket of darkness sprinkled with virtually endless warm, glistening sparkles. It always reminded P.J. of the sun sparkles from the crests of the wind-driven waves on a clear stream where he used to fish. The opportunities lay before him like unspoiled moments.

As he carefully laid down on the grass with the large crinkling bag of potato chips beside his head, P.J. ceremoniously began the process of licking each individual finger of the all traces of oil and salt, just like a cat cleaning its paws.

In the speed of a blink, a shooting star sped by and faded to his left as fast as it had appeared. The moment to appreciate passed and then one more flashed to his right. A few deep breaths later another streaked from one side of the universe to the other. P.J. just laid back astonished like his little brother would be at their neighboring town's fireworks celebration finale. Without moving his head, he reached around for the bag of chips only to find to his surprise and disappointment that it was empty. How sad. One more laser beam of light shot to his right and then one to his left. This shooting star show never got boring. Like a game of celestial speed billiards, the shooting stars seemed to sink into their black holes. He was getting good at anticipating where the next burst of light would come from.

Then P.J. locked his eyes onto one particular, magnificent pinpoint of light as it raced across the flat blackness from his left to his right when it stopped and suddenly changed direction. How puzzling. Then he heard a small but disturbing rustle coming from the bush across the yard. Wait a minute. *A shooting star can not suddenly turn directions,* he thought. *Why would there be an animal rustling in the bushes at this time of night?* Ever since his brother had hit him on the back of the head with that super hero mallet earlier that day caused his eyes and ears were just playing tricks on him. P.J. shook his head hard, like a wet dog drying himself, trying to clear the strangeness from his cloudy head.

Now back to the job at hand, thought P.J., hunting shooting stars, and just as quickly one by one the memories began to fade with each new shooting star. One short streaking flash to the left. One more to the right. The comfort of the familiar began to settle back into his chest. But then, after he'd taken a reassuring deep breath, it happened again. A long streak of whiteness suddenly turned and darted left as if it had hit a wall. Then, *smack*. P.J. was hit directly on the left cheek with a small but painful chunk of rock. In a blur of rage, P.J. swirled around, gripping his trusty, rusty scout flashlight, flooding a light beam into the trees in search of his soon-to-be-deceased little brother, or so he thought.

Thinking he was dreaming while awake, P.J. thought he saw a blur of some type of short, dark creatures dive into the bushes as fast as a Riley (our family dog) hid under the covers when he knew he did something very wrong. Without thinking, P.J. jumped into action. This proud "star warrior", after a quick super hero pose with fists to his sides, grabbed his sadly empty chip bag and his light wand (flashlight), and dove into the bushes with a burst of sheer adrenaline. Before he realized what he had done, he was lying in a flattened bush with outstretched arms and thinking his chip bag was full of nothing but air. Or is it? About to admit defeat, he looked up to see his bag was moving, and not so empty after all. He had actually caught the villain. Straightening himself up, he held the squirming, rattling bag with the top squished shut. Whatever it was, it would not get out. Victory was all his.

P.J. secured the plastic airtight sack tight at the top, leaving no room for his conquest to escape. The bag jerked and pulled repeatedly. This creature was kicking from inside the bag dangling from his outstretched arms straight in front of him. As his heartbeat slowed, his curiosity grew with every sudden kicking jolt. P.J. smiled to himself as he remembered when he had wrapped his little brother in his bed sheet, tying Liam to the bed post for having just woken P.J. with a splash of old aquarium water. P.J. thought, *Maybe he should set whatever this was loose in his sleeping brother's bed. That would teach him. The only problem with that is that they slept in the same room. Just when he was getting used to the rhythmic-kicking bag, it stopped. This self-energized captive was far too small to truly annoy his little brother.* Thoughts swept through him. *What if it died? What if it's a crazed squirrel that's lying in wait, ready to strike for his throat?*

He sat the now still bag on the grass in front of him. P.J. moved cautiously backwards and placed himself on the cool grass beside it. He looked tentatively at the crinkly sack. P.J. inched uncomfortably closer. Loosening his grip, the once-warrior carefully peered into the expanding opening, as if a bizarre lunch that his grandmother prepared for him awaited within. He had seen enough scary movies to know that this was just when the terrifying, boy-eating monster pops up and eats him in two bites. Drowning in visions, he opened the bag wider and wider until it was completely open. Still nothing. The curious adventurer with his knees tight to his chest then poked the bag with his foot and jumped back, waiting for the mayhem to ensue. Nothing. A second thrust with the bottom of his foot. Nothing.

P.J. grabbed the bottom corners of the weighted bag and flipped whatever was inside onto the clammy grass to end the suspense. Armed with his trusty flashlight/ninja fighting stick, he was also ready to bolt away for safety. Out rolled a squirrel...no a leprechaun...no a... He was as confused now as he had been earlier. The stout elf-life prisoner vigorously shook his head back and forth trying to shake sense into his abrupt predicament. Gradually he or it stood up, straightening himself in preparation of a formal presentation by brushing off the oil-soaked potato chip fragments. There he stood, about fifteen inches tall with normally confident eyes now sporting a slightly embarrassed expression.

"Who are you?", asked the mighty elfish stranger with one upturned bushy eyebrow,

Taken aback, P.J. replied, "Who are *you*?"

Clearing his throat, the peculiar yet distinguished captive proclaimed "I am Pinch, Proud member of the Grand Smidgeon Tribe."

"Smidgeon?" P.J. blurted.

Pinch was taken aback by this warrior's ignorance of his high stature in his world order but still tolerant because he was indeed his captive. "Can't you tell?", the mighty midget snorted, slightly insulted, "What are you?", he fired back at P.J. "and why do I smell like oily onions?" The once distinguished Pinch still kept brushing himself clean of the tiny crumbs that seemed to be stuck all over him. Pinch was annoyed until one speck brushed his lips and then stopped suddenly in appreciation, like when a puppy discovers peanut butter for the first time. "Hmmmmm."

A little curl grew at the end of P.J.'s boyish smile as the conquering boy warrior leaned forward politely. Bowing slightly, he said, "I am P.J. I live in that house." He pointed to the nearest building in the darkness, "I am a boy...". Interrupting himself then demanded, "Hey, wait a minute. I caught you in *my* trusty sour cream and onion potato chip super-size bag because you were messing up my shooting star show. Plus you hit ME with something, too". He gently pointed to his own now reddish cheek.

Now the smidgeon smirked knowingly in acknowledgement. The perplexed boy continued, "Why are you smirking?" Relaxing a little bit, Pinch continued stumbling over his words, "You believe in *shooting stars*?" The compact visitor answered, holding back a muffled snicker. "Why shouldn't I believe in *shooting stars*?" P.J. asked. Pinch now obliged answered, "Since you did indeed catch me. I am required to truthfully answer all of your questions and grant you any wishes until you release me of my obligation."

"Are you a leprechaun or something?", P.J. asked.

The proud Smidgeon quickly shifted from humble to annoyed, and snorted, "I told you I'm a Smidgeon."

Now, more confused than he had been before, P.J. cautiously backed up and sat down on a half-rotted stump and tried one more time, "With all due respect to you and your kind, I have never heard of a Smidgeon. Where are you from? How many of you are there? What makes Smidgeons unique? Why have I or any humans that I know never heard of you or seen you?", P.J. asked as if one long question.

Pinch sniffed out slightly in amusement, defusing his anger. Standing tall (for a Smidgeon that is), he puffed out his chest as if trying to answer every question in one long breath and began, "The Smidgeons are ancient noble beings. Many of us primarily live in the Northern Woodlands just north of here, but we've been known to frequent wherever humans are." Looking upward as if grabbing words from the air, he continued, "We live in the base of the finest oak and birch trees...snuggled safely between their extended root branches, and have done so for thousands of years. As for why you never see us, well...we don't want you to. It's that simple."

Not satisfied with that answer, P.J. blurted, almost offended, "Why don't you want us to see you?"

Pinch replied with a slightly embarrassed air. "We've seen and heard about what you humans do to the earth, trees and creatures that you say that you care about, like buffalo and whales. We figure that it's better for all of us to stay clear of you and let you think that you run everything."

P.J. leaning forward with excitement asked, "Why can I see you now?".

"Its part of our code of honor that if we are captured by any of you that in exchange we work as your servant for our release.

Of course, these wishes can only be those that affect your daily life, not for you to live forever or have every one love each other forever. Understand now?"

The inside of P.J.'s brain was swirling as fast as that time that Santa Claus first asked him what he wanted for Christmas, but he continued his questioning.

"Now tell me about why you laughed when I said that I believed in shooting stars?"

Pinch responded as if talking about something laughable, "See...stars are as big as our sun, just farther away," making sure to speak slowly enough for the human to follow his logic, "Sooo does it make sense for them to randomly start screeching across the universe for no apparent reason?" Pinch snickered to himself softly into his clenched right hand and as if saying a joke added,"- Maybe it's for your enjoyment."

P.J. acknowledged his point by nodding his head and adding, "but...."

As if not hearing him, the tiny teacher continued, "Smidgeons have long played a game called "fire flyby". Complete with exaggerated hand gestures, he explained, "You see, two of us sit in the tree tops across from each other. One has a glass jar of freshly captured fireflies. Do you know what they are?"

Baffled yet fascinated, P.J. answered, "Yes."

Pinch continues the lecture, "One Smidgeon carefully takes one of the fireflies with his fingertips out of his jar and tosses it. Occasionally humans look up into the dark skies and see one of these fireflies soaring from the treetops and call it what you call "a shooting star.""

"Okay, I guess I can understand that," P.J. said. "But that doesn't explain the second Smidgeon in the other tree."

"That's where the sport comes in. The other Smidgeon, usually me around here, holds a satchel...a small leather bag...with smidgeon fist-sized pieces of rock. The sport is to throw the rock directly at the firefly sailing by and hit it. Hit it and you win. It can take several nights to get one hit. Tonight", lifting his chin as if to pose for a portrait, with pride, Pinch reported, "I hit two of them. That's a record." Lowering his chin a little to see P.J.'s shock, "But as you already know, one of my hummers (pieces of rock) hit you by accident as it fell...Sorry about that", lowering his chin to his chest in embarrassment. "Then I was so excited doing my victory dance that I fell off of my tree branch and fell in the blueberry bushes, just to your right. Before I could regain my senses, you trapped me in that magical smelly, crinkly sack and here I am. I went from local hero to your humble servant in just a matter of seconds. Speaking of which, as I said before, I have to grant you wishes, and then you must let me go. With this fire flyby feat, they'll probably be throwing me a parade, or something. So let's get this over with..."

P.J. thought for a minute, with his right palm cupped under his chin, "I don't know where to begin."

With a mischievous twinkle in his eye, Pinch said, "Why not start with your brother, Liam?"

"Hmmm", P.J. said slowly, stroking the back of the freshly wounded cheek, "Maybe."

"Didn't he hit you with a stick today? ...What about the mess that he makes in your room?", Pinch blurted.

Those questions broke his concentration."Wait a minute. How do you know about our room being a mess?", P.J. asked.

"Your room is the stuff of legends. We tell our youngest children stories of your room, to scare them into behaving and cleaning their rooms. Plus, a couple of the hottest summer nights last year me and my friend, Dollop snuck into your room and spent the night in your closet. It's nice and cool in your house. Although," Pinch added, "even at our size, we had trouble fitting, there was so much junk in there."

P.J. asked, "Weren't you afraid of being caught?"

"Have you looked at your room? We could have probably hidden our entire village in there if we needed to, if they weren't so afraid.", Pinch defended.

"Okay, okay, I get your point. But that's Liam's fault. I wish I could teach him a lesson," P.J. said..

"Exactly. No problem. Your wish is my command. It will be taken care of," his servant answered. While pointing his bony somewhat hairy stub of a finger into the air in assurance, Pinch declared, "I've got an idea." Who would have known that's when these new friends were born.

As instructed, P.J. went back to bed, even though his heart was pounding with all of the excitement of this night. His head was still spinning with questions. He slipped into the bottom bed of his bunk bed to the gentle rustling of his annoying slob of a brother sleeping in the bed above him. Despite all of the excitement, P.J. fell asleep fairly fast as well.

Like clockwork, around 3 a.m., Liam (or "little Satan," as P.J. sometimes called him behind his mom's back), climbed methodically down his wooden side stairs backwards and, without opening his eyes more than a squint, waded through the dirty mounds of clothes out of the room to get a glass of water from the bathroom faucet next to the guinea pig cages. Awoken P.J. heard the faucet run, the glass' remaining water dumped into the sink and the serenade of the squeaking guinea pigs, begging for food and attention that once lay sleeping by the sink snug in their cage on the counter.

Liam trudged back through the ever-invading dirty clothes. Liam dragged his feet through the waves of dirty laundry as if he were walking through the shallow waves at that beach near Grandpa's house. It was almost like he was still dreaming. Still in that state between being asleep and awake, his left foot hit something. Something ...not clothes, and with some brief inspection with his toes, not a toy. He tried to push it away with his foot. No luck. It wouldn't budge.

Liam was trying to step over it, when, suddenly, the pile grabbed his ankle. He could feel something wrap tight ,like tentacles, around his ankle and hold him from going any further. He thought he was still dreaming. That was it. *This is a bad dream but still a dream.* His left eye then opened wide enough to look down into the murky darkness of the bedroom. There was a small, hairy hand gripped around his left ankle. Then a second stubby, yet strong, hand began reaching up from the now jostling floor of clothes. *This can't be happening.* Liam was beginning to convince himself of this until the second hand wrapped firmly around his right ankle and then both hands tugged sharply, sending him face-first onto the floor. *Luckily, it was well-padded by filthy mounds of laundry,* he thought.

Liam hit with such a thud that he woke himself completely up. His mind was immediately racing to blame his creepy older brother, when he saw P.J. still lying comfortably in the bed directly in front of him. *How could this be?* Liam had walked this path night after night and made it safely. Just when he tried to justify this as part of some weird dream, a snarling troll-like creature rose draped with the piles of fowl-smelling clothes as growled his name menacingly, "Llllllllllliiiiiiiiiiiaaaaaaaammmmmmm.

Lllllllliiiiiaaaaaaaammmmm. You will pay for what you have done. Lllllllliiiiiiaaaaaammmmm."

The creeping creature was covered in slightly-stained clothes including torn jeans that Liam had worn when he was a small kid. It's two saggy ears that were draped each in a different colored sock. This was peculiar yet terrifying, especially in the dark. With that Liam shot up on his feet in one leap and hurdled his "wooly" enemy in one fell swoop as the bureau. Liam darted and cleared the doorway, he shot a glance back at his brother, as if to say that *I wish you the best, but every kid for himself.*

Liam proceeded to stomp down the staircase muttering to himself all the way. He cleared the last few steps in one jump. He flung open the front door and bolted outside into the front yard, far away from the house. Liam stopped at the top of the driveway to pace back and forth and mumbled like that crazy man he had once seen on the subway.

Meanwhile back, in the bedroom, P.J. burst into fits of belly laughter that kept him curled up in uncontrollable spasms of joy.

Pinch was dancing wildly while still wearing the socks on his ears and inside-out underwear as a vest. Increasing with each high Russian-style dance kick step, Pinch started to laugh more. P.J., though, didn't realize that a bizarre thing happens when Smidgeons laugh. They fart. The louder P.J. and Pinch laughed, the louder Pinch farted. The more Pinch laughed, the more he farted. The more he farted, the more they both laughed. With the sounds and the sight of this crazy elf-like creature rolling on his floor while still laughing and farting, P.J. began to laugh more with every fart. The circle of odor-driven hysteria kept repeating and felt like it would never end. It wasn't that bad, though, because an even stranger fact is that Smidgeons' farts smell like fresh-baked apple pie, and P.J. liked apple pie.

It all came to a quick end when P.J.'s Dad stomped deliberately up the stairs and flung open his creaky wooden door, demanding "P.J., What did you do to your brother?" Hiding a knowing half-smile that might give him away, P.J. rubbed his eyes and said, "I didn't do anything Dad. I was sleeping".

His dad became suddenly distracted by the strong odor of baked apple pie. Sniffing at the air. He turned and walked out the door and yell down the stairs, "Dear, do we have any apple pie?! I really could go for some apple pie."

A short time later as night fell, the excitement and the odor faded. Liam slept on the floor of Mom and Dad's room. Pinch settled in for a few hours of sleep covered comfortably by a bed of dirty clothes and a job well done. P.J. closed his eyes still smiling and drifting off.

Sunlight broke in through the window. P.J. woke with the strong feeling that someone was watching him. The memory of his new little hairy friend was still fresh. He had so much more to ask him. Confusion set in though, as he lifted his eyelids to see his life-sized little brother standing right in front of his face with his arms folded. Liam yelling through his teeth, "What did you do and why aren't you scared of the monster that was in our room yesterday?" P.J. knew Liam will tell anyone he never gets scared but he might get "concerned" over things that might eat him in the middle of the night.

"Well?", Liam interrogated. P.J. started to roll face-up on his back in annoyance, but then decided that he needed to savor every drop of his brother's distress, for as long as it would last.

Not letting up, Liam added, "Well?" accented with a lowering of his eye brows. Then, as if by an electric shock, P.J. shot up and started to look all around for Pinch. Liam couldn't have seen him. *Liam can't see him. That would destroy every morsel of the fun of having a Smidgeon friend.*

Liam stood waiting impatiently for an answer as P.J. looked over his own head, around his feet and towards the closet. P.J. stood up, stalling and distracted. "Hmmmm....Well...I don't know what you are talking about. I...I...was sleeping throughout the whole thing...Whatever it was."

P.J. circled the room, trying to discreetly lift away piles of clothes with his feet, looking for his newfound little friend. Besides, he remembered that Smidgeons have been hidden for a thousand years, so how could his lame little brother could ever see one.

Just as P.J. thought he gotten away with it, and Liam started to turn towards the door, There came a sound. A lip-smacking, finger-licking, lip-licking sound began to waft from under P.J.'s bed. P.J. started to panic a little. He faked a sneeze to cover the sounds, but it didn't work.

Liam turned and asked, "What was that?"

"What?"

"That noise...like an animal licking his lips...." Liam turned his back towards the door in preparation for a look under their beds.

P.J. banged on the top of the bed to emphasize his point. "I don't know what you're talking about!", he said loudly, hoping this would warn Pinch to just keep quiet.

But Liam definitely had heard it. He fell to his knees and then lay flat on the floor, crawling over to the edge of the bed's base. He inched up and lifted the bed cover that hung over the edge. He squished one eye to focus (and with a little fear) even harder as he lifted the cover to expose the floor under their beds wondering if he would be eaten alive right there and then. P.J. horrified at the invasion of privacy, slid to the side of the bed and tried to sneakily push down the cover that Liam was raising. The bed cover battle went back and forth, until Liam blurted, "Just one look, and I'll leave."

P.J. reluctantly relented, thinking that Pinch had to be smart enough to disappear, or turn into something that looked innocent..

"I can't believe it," Liam calmly stated.

"What?" PJ said, still trying to act innocent.

Liam pulled out a musty little league baseball cap. The dust bunnies and lint on it were so thick that it looked like a hat covered in gray cotton-candy. "I thought I lost this years ago!" Liam looked like a little kid who had just got a new toy, quickly forgetting that he was crying for just thirty minutes before.

He started bringing the cap up to lips to blow off the dust bunnies when a tiny hand reached out from under the bed cover to reach for it. Striking with the speed of a cobra, the hand grabbed the hat and dragged it back under the bed. Liam and P.J. were both in shock, but for different reasons. Then the lip-smacking, lip-licking and satisfied moaning started again with new vigor. P.J. fell back, pressing his hands against his head in frustration. Liam dove face first under the bed cover, his outstretched arms seeking the previously-forgotten treasure, his old cap. He got his fingertips on it, but once again it was yanked from his grip. Then he felt the slap of a tiny hand on the back of his hand, as if saying, "Back off, this is mine."

Now the battle was on. Liam, with all of the fury that he could muster, dove back under. The tug-of-war pulled back and forth, back and forth, back and forth. This was becoming an epic battle of strength and commitment with some unseen force from under their bed. Liam would not lose. He could not lose.

With one final pull, Liam scored the cap but with so much force that he sailed backwards, rolling somersaults until he lay

against his clothes dresser. He'd won. He got the cap. It was his...
forever...again.

But then something even stranger occurred to him. He noticed
that the cap was clean. Clean as if it was fresh out of a washing
machine, or a used dinner dish just cleaned by their Lab puppy,
Riley. Wait a minute. What was that thing that had tried to take his
now-favorite cap? Liam crawled like a cautious lioness towards
its prey on the grasslands towards the scene of the unknowing
victim. When he got there, he sheepishly lifted the hanging bed
cover edge with his thumb and forefinger and one foot poised
towards the door.

In the darkness of the abyss that lay underneath his bed, he
heard a sound of finger licking and lip smacking. He tried his
hardest to focus on the sound but all he saw was darkness but the
sound...the sound kept going. It drove him crazy. Liam reached
up to grab his floor lamp by the base and slowly lowered it without removing his stare from the darkness. Liam lost his grip, and
the lamp fell to the floor sideways behind him and shot a beam of
light that washed over the darkness.

He was suddenly three feet away from the cutest yet odd-
est-looking creature he had ever seen. This thing reminded him of
one of those almost hairless dogs that he'd seen on that "World's
Strangest Animals" television show. Liam tilted his head to one
side in amazement. The creature, as if in a mirror, did the same.
He tilted his head back and "the thing" tilted its head back, too.

Liam couldn't figure out whether to laugh, cry or scream. The
two wary warriors locked stares. It was just like when P.J. and he
would have staring contests on long drives with their family. All
the while, the odd little fellow continued to lick and suck at his
fingertips as if to get every last drop. Pinch said ,softly through his
fingertips a muffled, "Hi."

That broke the tension. Liam smacked the ground with his fist. He never lost that game with P.J. Liam was still champion (in his eyes anyway). A curl broke out on the corner of Pinch's "grinch-iest" smile. Liam matched it with one of his own. Liam rolled comfortably on his side and put his hand under his head. Pinch broke the verbal silence again and asked, "Do you have more of that fuzzy stuff? It tastes like candy...only better." Liam asked, "You mean the dust bunnies?" Pinch, now more interested than ever, replied, "Dust bunnies. I like dust bunnies. They taste like sweet clouds of perfection."

Liam, half-disgusted yet half-intrigued, said, "You know, in just a few days they'll grow right back here." Pinch let out a wistful sigh of contentment, "I'll just wait here then until this "candy garden" treats grow back. Can you close that flap?" Liam started to, and then burst out with, "No. What are you doing here? Why are you here? What are you?", so fast that Pinch thought it was one question.

"Wait a minute," Pinch pleaded, "Master P.J.!! Master P.J.!"

P.J. answered, "Yes?"

"Is it okay for me to tell him?"

Liam shot P.J. a glance that said without a word, *You know, you're my favorite brother and if you let him tell me, I'll forgive you for any wrongdoings that you may have done to me...ever...probably.*

"Yeah, okay,." P.J. answered. "Go ahead and tell him."

And so Pinch did just that deep into the night. Liam just listened until he fell fast asleep.

They woke the next morning as the sunlight poked through their window and stabbed straight into P.J.'s sleepy eyes. He wiped his eyes so hard he still saw multi-color blurred images for a while after he got up. Liam lay sprawled on his back, wedged in between two of the largest heaps of smelly clothing. Curled into a ball, Pinch snuggled with his head on Liam's chest. All was new and glorious with the world. P.J. breathed extra deeply, as if to absorb the goodness inside and out. This was the best he had felt in years. Nothing could ruin this. Or so he thought.

The window was cracked open a little and he could hear the sound of the notorious band of bike-riding thugs. They instantly caused tensions to rise and people to leave wherever they went. P.J. flinched with every sound of the bike tires sliding sideways over the asphalt. It was like a band-aid was being ripped out with every slide. The "pure evil" bullies circled the top of their long driveway like vultures waiting for their prey to die...and that could be shortly, if P.J. and Liam went outside right now. What hurt the most was it was a beautiful day and they would have to deal with their parents. They now had to pretend that they wanted to stay inside and play video games when they would rather feel the wind whipping through their tousled hair as they sped along the streets on their pedal-powered "rocket ships". What a waste.

P.J. let a grunt of disappointment so loud that it woke up both Liam and Pinc. Liam stretched out and looked over in sheer happiness of finding a new friend...no matter how peculiar he might look and even smell. Pinch had a distinctive musky, very outdoorsy aroma about him. Liam liked it.

Liam looked at PJ and said, "What's wrong P.J.?"

"They're back," is all he had to say, and their innocent bliss drifted right out the ajar window.

Confused, Pinch asked, "Am I missing something?"

P.J. pointed out the half-opened window to a swarming brood of bikers perched at the top of their driveway...waiting...taunting.

"They don't look so tough.", Pinch snorted.

"They are," P.J. replied reluctantly with a hard swallow.

Pinch confidently stated, "I could help you take care of them. Would you like that?"

"I don't think you understand. They have stuffed both of us in lockers. Tossed us up into trees. Given us "wedgies" so bad, I couldn't walk right for a week. And that's just the start. I came home one day from school with them on the bus and found 3 pieces of cooked spaghetti and 2 pencil erasers in my underwear....my underwear...my underwear!"

Pinch interrupted, "But you didn't have a friend like me."

Hearing that declaration, a twinkle came back in P.J.'s eye and Liam straighten up a little. With his most villainous grin, P.J. rubbed his palms together, like he was trying to start a fire, and broke into a contented "hmmmmmmm." They shot ideas of conquest faster than popcorn popping on an open fire all night long.

It's 8:58 on Sunday Morning and two minutes until impact. This will soon to be known as the *"Battle of the Bullies"* or the *"Decline of the Evil Empire."*, thought Liam. There P.J. and Liam stood—two modern-day warriors, at the crest of the driveway battleground waiting...waiting for their destiny. These two mighty soldiers each ceremoniously and carefully adorned themselves with street hockey gear armor in anticipation of this grand moment. Padded elbow pads for when arm to arm combat became the only option. Well-worn fingerless leather gloves to ensure a better grip of the weapons of choice. For Liam, hanging from his left belt loop was a used household toilet plunger. This would be perfect as an evil-fighting sword and a deflector of flying munitions. Then when he was eventually victorious, he could humiliate his conquest by placing the often used, disgusting rubber suction end over the nose and mouth of the defeated in ultimate triumph and shout,"Take that!"

Liam's right hand firmly gripped his trusty slingshot, which he traded a "troubled youth" for in the darkest part of the playground two weeks ago. He gave away his entire stash of candy that he built from months of visits with his grandmother. It was worth it. In his bulging pocket were the finest oval stones that had collected for this exact purpose. On his head was a once-cool looking bicycle helmet adored with lightning bolts that he had always sworn made him ride faster.

To his right, stood his big brother, P.J. braced for the skirmish of a lifetime. He, too, wore mismatched elbow pads – topped, though, with a blue metallic bicycle helmet (slightly too small for his head) glistening in the new day rising sun as if blinding the enemy was a part of P.J.'s grand arsenal of chosen weapons. P.J. though went in a different direction with a dull scout Swiss army knife stuffed securely into his right pocket for easy access. This old-school weapon had 3 knives (which he can not open anymore), a fork, a corkscrew, scissors and unfolded surprises that he had yet to need or use. Hanging from his left belt loop was a personally carved mallet of mass destruction. He had sculpted this wooded weapon of choice from one large block of pine; it had taken him one whole summer. This weapon of mass destruction was light and nimble but packed the strength that Thor, the god of war, would be proud. Emblazoned into the oak handle was "P.J.," so there would be no question of who was the rightful owner and craftsman.

The two protectors of "all that is good" stood there still like samurais counting the seconds with each breath. Off to their left stood two curious onlookers, two harmless-looking squirrels namely Pinch and a new unknown onlooker. Pinch and the two boys looked over at this new unexpected visitor with slight confusion that would not deter from their battle at hand. Pinch sat back on his solid squirrel hindquarters and chomped anxiously on his newfound acorn, as if devouring a bucket of buttery popcorn while watching an exciting adventure movie. This adventure was going to unfold right in front of him and, with a little luck, might even include him and his ingenious battle plans. Off in the distance grew the sounds of what sounded like an angry swarm of 70 pound wasps that just had their nest shattered by a rock. The murmur of future criminals grew closer and the troubling sounds of spinning tires over the sand-laced asphalt street lead to this final battleground. Were they ready? Well, It was too late to think about it now. It was 9 a.m. on the dot. The bullies "torment tour" arrived every weekend day just like clockwork. The motley trouble-making tribe turned their rear tires in a skidding stop in unison expecting the sound of crunching hopes that they heard every weekend day. Fear is what fed them. But this time it was different somehow. This time their one synchronized ballet-like movement every rear tire continued to slide. They couldn't stop. The ground was covered in motor oil. Just like Pinch planned. Their bikes spun uncontrollably onward past their intended destination. They just couldn't stop, even when they slammed down their other foot down to brace their fall, only to have that foot slip along with the bike. The bikes and their confused riders slide sideways for another 10 feet before coming to a sudden stop on a patch of dry road. One rider after the other spilled on top of their bikes. The bikes flipped over until they lay in a scattered mess across the dead-end street asphalt. One bully methodically picked up his bike along with his broken ego and walked it on the sidewalk past the others, limping and trying not to cry in front of his fellow thugs. Pinch began to bend over laughing in sheer admiration of his handiwork and how easy that this was going to be. As he did this, little "bum-burps" (as P.J.'s mother called farts) came out. The mysterious squirrel, sitting next to Pinch, suddenly tensed up and looked over at Pinch. Pinch thought, *Hey, lighten up, it's just a little gas. It happens.* The squirrel didn't seem to be amused or even willing to tolerate it. Meanwhile, the band of brooders began to rise from their ashes of embarrassment and assemble around their leader. Rising up and shaking off the confusion, each gang member lined up behind like Canadian geese in a "flying V" formation and ready for battle.

Their leader, Snort, locked eyes with P.J.. Local legend had it that he was called "Snort" because if you heard him snort that's the last sound you will ever hear again. Snort knew that if you take down the tallest and oldest member of any enemy's troop, you will win even quicker and easier. The only thing that Snort didn't know is that things were different today. P.J. knew no fear today. He had a new secret weapon, Pinch. And looking down to his left, he had a brother who was living out a "videogame warrior" dream.

P.J. gave his best Spartan leader growl, trying to hold back a leer of amusement from the oil slick that the three of them had made just an hour before from all of the used motor oil that Dad never bothered to throw away. P.J. matched Snort's intensity with his own memories of this "walking demon"'s past antics that had caused him so many sunny days locked in the cell of his room, in fear of the torment and pain. It was all now bubbling to the surface. This was P.J.'s last stand (and maybe the world's last chance at victory over evil), and he knew it. P.J. tried not to break the gaze of his opposition's shark-like stare. He dared not look down at the oil-drenched rope that lay in wait for his command. P.J. finally broke his stare, turned his head and winked at Pinch.

Pinch sprang into action. He sprinted to the end of the rope near him, grabbed it with his teeth and pulled it with all his Smidgeon might. He leaped to the other side of a "just as mighty" oak and proceeded to yank tight and then to wrap the rope around the base of the tree. Pinch sped in and out of their legs back to the other side. Then Pinch finished the secure scout knot to the tree on the other side of the street, just like P.J. had taught him. This is a knot that's so tight it would never be budged. At the same time, Snort and his gang watched as rope rose from the oil-soaked road to encircle and quickly wrap around their ankles and tug them back down to the ground that they just brushed themselves off from. But this time, their rear-ends were covered with old motor oil and their legs lay shackled together by twisted rope and some sort of sailor knot. They tried to lift themselves, each one looking more like a calf just tied at a rodeo than a fearsome warrior. P.J. looked at Liam who grinned ear to ear. P.J. yelled "Hold!", instructing Liam to stay still.

The thugs lifted themselves in unison on their sides to rise to the feet. In one movement of the tightening rope, they fell again. This time, they landed face-first into the slimy blackness that now appeared to have been leaking directly out of their veins. Drenched with gooey black liquid, the seemingly defeated tormentors sat up and began to calmly unwrap their shins from the rope snare traps set for them.

This is when the losing bully boys should have just collected their bikes and gone home, but, as P.J. had suspected, it would not be that easy. "Wallop!", screamed Snort, as if on fire from the inside. Just then, the seemingly innocent squirrel sitting so calmly besides Pinch hopped over and quickly chewed the rope from the tree which loosened it so that each of the boys could maneuver free.

Pinch quickly realized that he should have gone with his hunch. He knew that squirrel had looked too smart. It was in his eyes… too focused, too sharp. That was a Smidgeon. Squirrels were like caffeinated monkeys that dart continuously from tree to tree looking for their next nut. This one was different.

Could it be?, he thought. That must be why these gangsters have been so unbeatable. Pinch smacked his head with the palm of his hand and thought, *How could I be so stupid?*

Just then the squirrel somersaulted through the air as if it were in slow-motion with a majestic ease of a flying squirrel, with Pinch as his destination. *Oh, oh.,* Pinch thought. He gave a quick glance over to P.J. to let him know that the boys were going to have to fend for themselves right now. He was about to have the fight of his life...for his life.

P.J. had no time to be confused, because the group of oil-soaked zombies rose and slopped forward, dripping blackness wherever they stepped. "To the fort!", P.J. yelled. Liam turned and P.J. led them to his lair, their backyard tree house. It was built with their dad one summer ago. It had since begun to fall apart, but it would provide the sanctuary that they needed. The enraged gaggle of thugs built speed, as they shed oil. They were chasing so fast after their new prey (P.J. and Liam), he thought for a moment that they might actually burst into flames. No such luck. The hungry for revenge hunters nearly caught up to P.J. and Liam, Followed by oil-soaked stains on the newly cut lawn.

Liam was first. He jumped clear onto the third rung of the rope ladder to the tree house. P.J., just a blink behind, hopped on the first rung of the wiggly rope ladder. Liam reached the top and was already hunched over, ready to pull up the ladder, as P.J. hurled himself off onto the floor of tree house. One the creeps' hands grabbed P.J's ankle, but Liam grabbed his trusty toilet-strained plunger, and stretched out, and stuck it smack right onto the disgusted creep's face. The mortified slug had to let go of P.J. to remove this smelly rubber suction device from his already foul face. Then Liam hesitated, his hand on the ladder. "Where's Pinch?"

"He signaled for us to go on without him."

"Here we go", they said together, as they both lifted the ladder just out of the reach of the incensed marauders, who now circled the base of the tree just 10 feet below. They continued to bark at each other, like a pack of humiliated, slippery wolves. The bullies circled and weaved snake-like, planning their next cruel act. With his heart still pounding, P.J. gazed down into the "fire in their eyes" and the "hollowness in the souls". He fell back flat on the floor.

Liam was still huffing and puffing when he caught P.J.'s eye and he pointed with his eyes to an old feather mattress that they had tossed up here to give a softer place to lay during their marathon games of poker with the neighborhood kids. Liam's eyes grew larger suddenly. "I got a great idea", he said. P.J. rolled back on his back and nodded for him to do whatever he wanted. Liam saw these war-dancing grunts below him, still covered in motor oil, like an old three stooges show that they used to watch with their dad, and knew what would deliver the final knock-out blow to their egos. "P.J., can I borrow your knife please?" Liam asked. "Don't worry, I won't lose it."

P.J. dug out his rusted knife and handed it to Liam, who swiftly proceeded pull out whatever he could get unstuck to drive it straight into the heart of the old feather mattress. P.J. sprang up and said, "Let me help."

The gang of darkness still buzzed and circled below, making the perfect target. Liam declared, "1,2,3—Go!"

With that, the bullies all looked up as the feathers poured on top of them, sticking to the motor oil. They now looked like a flock of half-plucked chickens that had just gone through an oil tornado. Their air of superiority was now officially gone.

Liam gave a content high-five to his big brother and fellow

warrior. They could now lie back down. Success. One by one, the fractured gang began to splinter off, limp back up to their bikes, and waddled home, leaving dragging tracks of blackness and occasional feather behind them. Never to forget this day.

Worst of all, every kid in the neighborhood began to leave their home with growing waves of laughter and applause as the bullies, defeated, headed back home where they belonged. Even Snort slinked away walking his bike beside him all the way down the street and yelled back, "Wallop" you are on your own!".

The two exhausted, victorious warriors slowly lowered the ladder and cautiously made their way to the front yard to see for themselves the source all of this joy. As they began to savor the victorious celebration, like that one last potato chip, they saw off in the corner of their eye, two squirrels feverishly spinning, twirling, hurling, screeching at each other. It was a battle to the death. "Pinch!", the boys both bellowed as they dove to break them apart, not knowing really which one was which. Each boy grabbed one of the grayish blurs and crammed it into each of the old leaf bags that were left on the side yard. The seemingly spinning motion forced them to roll back down the hill in two undulating heaps. They were fighting like brothers fight though, with passion but not really trying to hurt each other. The melee finally stopped as the boys separated the bags and the two determined, rivaling rodents. Catching his breath, P.J. heard a muffled voice coming from his bag, "P.J., is that you? You already caught me once. You know this is getting a little embarrassing. You know that you can't get more wishes, or anything."

Liam, on the other hand, had captured the enemy Smidgeon. Liam now knew how this whole "capture and get wishes" thing worked (if this was indeed a Smidgeon). Liam stood and declared to the still writhing bag, "You are now mine and have to do whatever I say". One last punch for accentuation from inside the bag outward and the bag contents submitted, "Okay, my lord."

"I could get used to like that type of talk," Liam said to himself. Preparing to release his captive, Liam asked his brother, "You're sure about this, right?"

He lifted the black plastic bag off of his new fuzzy genie-like friend. This Smidgeon stood slowly and regally trying to muster any type of dignity of being captured yet again by these creepy human beings. He dusted himself off seemingly unaware that others were watching. The creature thought to himself, *Looking presentable was the only option, right now*. He began muttering with his chin down, "My name is Dollop. I am the King of the Smidgeons and I am humbly at your service, master."

Liam now felt a little bad. "You don't have to call me master. Mr. Liam would be fine." Then he added, "I thought that your name was Wallop?"

"That's just what those low-life Cretins called me. They thought that Dollop was too wimpy, or something."

"Well, I like Dollop better anyway," Liam replied.

"Me, too, Mr. Liam".

Liam had a new friend and dream maker of his own and he couldn't be happier. "Dollop, do you like dust bunnies, too?"

Trying to keep his composure, Pinch sat up. "Did someone say 'dust bunnies'?"

P.J. and Liam sat back and proceeded to peel off their sweaty battle gear piece by piece as slowly as they began to recount the story of their recent victory. Pinch and Dollop followed them as they headed back to their fort to discuss the day's events. After they climbed the wiggling rope ladder one at a time, they crawled and collapsed onto their backs, one by one. These four weary soldiers lay back staring blankly at the worn wood ceiling, the boys tried to flush the bad memories that had haunted them for so long. As they savored this moment, they heard random bikes being released from houses throughout the neighborhood. One by one, each bike rider seemed to chip at the once common silence. With each child in the neighborhood's spinning wheels, you could hear buzzing murmurs that reminded them of days long since past and almost forgotten. The flood gates of hope now led to laughter in the streets and fun in the air.

Liam suddenly breathed in deep, almost gasping. With a full chest of air, he turned his head toward Dollop and asked, "So... how did you get caught by the bullies anyway?". Dollop tilted his head to one side, looking back at Liam, "Which time?"

"There was more than one time?", Liam asked.

Dollop let out a deeper breath and answered, "To be a true leader, sometimes you have to take chances." A slight hesitation stopped him from continuing. The hesitation led to a lion-sized yawn. The yawn made him turn to his side and curl up in a more comfortable position. Dollop tried to continue, but his words seem to fade into mumbles and soon into sporadic polite snores of royalty. The excitement of the battle was just too much.P.J. and Liam just laid face up just listening to the whirring of bike wheels and kids laughing outside. Word quickly spread and the believers took to the streets. The stirrings only slowed as darkness fell. In the darkness, the victorious warriors scooped up their exhausted new friends. They all marched quietly back to the house through the cellar, up the stairs and into the safety of their room.

This was the best day ever...or so they thought.

TWO

⟶≫— —≪⟵

School Time

The next sounds that the boys heard were Mom and Dad yelling from out on the front lawn. They were discussing loudly about how those little thugs made such a mess with oil, rope and gravel all over the street. Mom exclaimed, "Someday someone's just going to have to do something out them". A devilish beam of pride came across P.J. and Liam's faces with the realization of what they had done. Liam turned to a waking P.J. and said, in a loud whisper, "Can you believe it? They think that the mess that we made was the bullies' fault. This just keeps getting better." Liam looked to his left to see Dollop laying on his back with his mouth open and a milky green slime dribbling out of the corner of his mouth. Liam's abrupt movement was so sudden that both Dollop and Pinch were shaken awake.

Suddenly stomping and seemingly annoyed footsteps rose up the stairs and ended with their door shooting open wide. "Time to get up for school, guys!" Dad always had a way of being tough but reassuring at the same time. Even though he talked from the doorway, he never really looked in. It didn't matter, though—Pinch and Dollop had vanished. "Boy, they are good," thought P.J.

The brothers started to look around quickly to see if they could find them, but the search was interrupted by Dad sticking his head back in. "Come on boys, move it."

Each boy picked up "new" clothes and a hair brush off the floor and proceeded to the door while still dressing, flattening their wild hair and looking around at the same time. "Come on Liam, gotta go," P.J. muttered. Liam, too tired to disagree, followed close behind him.

Like the focused zombies that they saw in the movie, that Dad let them see last week, they shoveled in their pancakes devoid of any emotion. Bite by Bite. Looking around with every bite to see if the world had changed. Mom kissed them on the top of their heads and scooted them from their squeaky chairs and towards the door, as only moms can do. Their bodies marched towards the door but their heads bobbed up and down unknowingly, looking for their new friends. With each step up the driveway, they silently began to wonder, was it just an amazing dream?

They reached the crest of the driveway. Both turned the corner to see a growing crowd of kids at the bus stop. The animated kids were all talking with hands and arms waiving telling exciting stories to each other like something cool had just happened.

Deirdre was the first to see them. She told her brother, Mikey, and soon every head stared directly at them. Liam looked behind them to see if a scary monster was coming up behind them. Then Mikey turned and started to run to them and soon everyone else followed. It was like a swarm of bees that just discovered who smashed their hive. They buzzed, swirled, walked and then ran at full speed towards P.J. and Liam. The boys looked at each other trying to figure out which way to run for their lives when they saw this crowd was smiling, patting them on the back and even cheering.

Thinking fast, P.J.'s yelled, "Red Light!" just like in the game "Red Light, Green Light", and the crowd of his oncoming mob of friends screeched to a halt in front of him. The boys looked back and forth at each other and spoke without saying a word, as only brothers can do.

Liam thought, *This was just too much.* Each boy had a plan in their head, P.J. would dive over the rock wall and Liam would head over a nearby hill, past the small statue of Buddha and into the woods that overlook the road. P.J. soon realized they meant them no harm. Then yelled, "Green Light" and soon their new fans quickly engulfed him.

Cheering. Chanting. Jumping in place. The two brothers were swept up in the upcoming wave of joy. *What is happening?* Liam was overwhelmed. The distinctly taller P.J. enjoyed it but seemed to be looking for a way out over their new admirers' heads. The swirling mass of happiness actually lifted them up. First by their legs, then onto their shoulders. The two breached like rejoicing whales from the moving mass to gasp for air as if they were submerged but now they were free. *Or were they?*

Liam thought he was in one of his favorite dreams when he was crowned King of all the Primates and carried off to their secret lair where they would play games and eat bananas forever. Just as quickly, he snapped out of it. P.J. yelled to Liam while they bounced on the shoulders of the neighborhood kids, "They're taking us to the bus stop!". The chants became clearer. "No More Snort! No More Snort! No More Snort!"

As if they had ordered a personal limo, their school bus pulled up the stop. The bus driver, Dale scratched his beard, confused by the chant, but he had heard stranger things. They all boarded,. The driver closed the door behind them all and drove on his next appointed rounds.

Idolizing eyes were fixed on their newly-crowned champions. Eager faces with chins planted on the top of the double seats were all positioned to best listen to the tale of how it had all happened. The victorious boys were still shaken by the whole tornado of excitement that surrounded them. P.J. said humbly, "It was nothing. We just told Snort and his gang to get lost. Then, they left." The eager faces seem to deflate a little until, out of the corner, came the voice of Deirdre saying, "I heard that you two took on the entire gang and kicked their butt." She seemed a little embarrassed for using the word "butt."

Liam, seeing that he was losing his fame, quickly sat up and added, "We thought with two of us and eight of them that it was a fair fight. We just did what we had to do. We told them to stop tormenting the neighborhood and leave us alone." Seeing that his audience's attention was restored, he said, "The gang of bullies didn't seem to want to go, so P.J. and I had to insist. Then, when that didn't work, we had to use our best samurai moves." Liam chopped the air with the edges of his knife-like hands, "Then we battled with our backs to each other. Bullies charged from all directions as if they were possessed by the devil. We just..." he looked over at Deirdre, "...had to kick their butts."

The kids in the bus started to stand up in excitement as Liam described the exciting battle punch by punch, blow by blow. Each bus rider got caught up in every swing in the adventure, just as if they were there. Liam stood up and started to swing his arms, acting out every action. Even P.J. got caught up in the moment, adding, "We kicked their butts!" every time Liam would pause in his telling his "mostly-true" tall tale.

It was so much more fun telling the story than being in it...a lot less terrifying, anyway. Just when they hit a fever pitch with the story, the bus jerked to a stop and the door whipped opened.

Out poured a wave of their disciples, full of new details that they would add onto. New spins of the conquest broke open into the school, spreading the word of the victory. P.J. and Liam the bus left last, flinging their heavy backpacks over their shoulders and marching off into the school like they owned it.

The hallways were packed solid. No matter which way they went, it seemed like everyone was pushing against them. It was like they were salmon trying desperately to go upstream to their homerooms. To make it even tougher, the entire time the boys were getting congratulation pats on the back.

Only Smash, Ziplock and the entire middle school football team pushed against and thru the waves. Their gang tormented to their entire school daily. They proudly stuffed kids into lockers, flipped other students' books onto the floor, lifted kids up by the scruff of their neck from "their" seats and tossed them to the floor with their books. Today, Smash and company formed their favorite football "wedge formation" and plowed through any hallway chaos. Wherever they went they left a wake of broken spirits. This muscled-ball of badness whacked the worshippers that surrounded Liam and P.J., knocking them to the floor without so much as a "Sorry" or "Oops."

"I hate those guys," muttered P.J. to Liam.

The school bell rang and everyone instantly cleared the halls.

P.J. made it to the closing door of his homeroom just as the bell ended. That was close. He started towards his seat, trying to be unnoticed that he was last to sit down. Every eye in the room was fixed on him. He slid into his seat flooded in a wave of murmurs. Even the teacher gave him a little wink, and she didn't really like him. P.J. slid off his hefty backpack, took out his notebook and got right to work. What a day. Little did he know that this was just the beginning.

Liam, meanwhile, was enjoying every moment of this new-found fame. He stood in the doorway of his homeroom with his arms outstretched, inviting applause. And he got it. Liam didn't even notice the teacher staring at him. Liam high-fived and fist-bumped his way to his back-row seat. He eventually sat down and squished his backpack in between himself and the pony-tailed girl that he liked who sat right in front of him.

Liam's brain was racing. He didn't hear a thing anyone said, including the teacher. Liam found himself staring straight ahead when the raven-haired girl, *Monica*, in front of him, turned around and gave him a knowing nod, as if to acknowledge that she liked him too. He nodded back, figuring maybe this had something to do with his newfound fame. When she did it again, she ran her hand through her ponytail and flung it over her shoulder, as if it was getting caught on something.

Liam said instinctively, "Sorry," even though he had no idea what was going on. He stared straight ahead blankly when suddenly, and for seemingly no good reason, she half spun around and now getting annoyed and said softy, "Would you stop doing that?"

He again said, "Sorry?" as a reflex, just like when you say "gesundheit" when someone sneezes.

What is going on? Liam thought. He sat fixated on her silky black ponytail, swinging back and forth, as if he was hypnotized.

Then he snapped out of it, when he saw a tiny furry arm reaching out of his slightly unzipped backpack, the hand gently stroking the silky strands. Then the outstretched hand started whacking at the ponytail, like it was a toy being dangled in front of a curious kitten. Too much to resist, I guess. Back and forth went Liam's head as if he were watching a tennis game. Then, with one deliberate wind up and follow-through, the scrawny arm smacked the pony tail so hard that it actually spun around in a circle.

Monica whipped around just as quickly, void of any patience, and yelled in her best whisper, "I said, STOP IT!" Liam tried to flash his best dimples, but soon slinked into a submissive ball of shame in his seat. "Sorry!," Liam answered while his back-of-the-room friends snickered.

Once she had turned back to face the teacher, he had a lightning bolt of anger that almost made him jump out of his seat, rip Dollop out of his backpack by his stubby arm and commence screaming at him. But, by the time, he reached down to grab Dollop's arm, it was gone. The backpack was fully zipped. Every other boy in the back row said, "Way to go, Liam", while giving him the thumbs up sign of approval. Liam forced a smile and sat back, as if he had planned this all along, and swallowed his anger and embarrassment. His mind started racing again. How did Dollop get in the backpack? Why did he smack *Monica's* ponytail? Time flew and the teacher squawked. Just as quickly, the bell rang.

Liam carefully picked up his secret cargo, said another sincere apology to *Monica,* and followed the rush of bodies as they poured into the hallway. Halfway down the hall, Liam spotted P.J.

"PJ!", he yelled. "P.J., I have something I need to tell you." P.J. was so focused on getting to his next class that he waved and politely ignored Liam.

"P.J.!".

No response.

P.J. entered his favorite class, "Science" with Mr. Baldo, and his eyes quickly locked in on Mr. Baldo's Bunsen burner in full flame. P.J. and his friends let out a not-so-subtle, "COOL!" as they strolled in. Pinch sniffed gently thru the zipper from inside the closed backpack to figure out what the fuss was. P.J. sat in his favorite seat, next to the window on Mr. Baldo's right hand side, for a close-up view. He swung around and sat down fascinated, never losing sight of the flames. He placed his backpack just behind his all-in-one seat/desk and braced for a fun science class. Pinch settled in by curling up and resting against the books in his bag. It was more snug than tight.

Mr. Baldo took beakers and glass cups, and filled them with all sorts of solutions. Cool blues ones. Hot pink ones. Some even sizzled. For his grand finale, Mr. Baldo mixed the blue and the pink and the green with some vinegar. It started to bubble. Then the bubbles rose so high, so fast that they started to pour over the top of the large glass container. It almost exploded. The whole class gasped as this Science his final act of the class. You could hear the sizzling, you could see the lava-like foam overflowing out of the glass' edge. Then a strong scent of apple pie wafted over the entire room. P.J. snapped out of his trance with a quick memory of what that smell meant with Smidgeons. From deep within his backpack, P.J. could hear a snickering, as if someone were trying to hold back laughter. He first thought he was imagining it. Somehow it sounded like Dollop. *But what would Dollop be doing here? He's at home, resting.* The sniffling soon turned into muffled laughs. This sound continued to get more noticeable as the smell got stronger.

Mr. Baldo ended his presentation to a round of applause (as much as you would ever expect to get in a school). Wait a minute. The apple pie smell was getting stronger but this time from behind him. P.J. followed the growing smell with his keen nose. He heard muffled laughter, along with what sounded like farts. He was sure everyone would notice. But they didn't.

As the school bell rang loudly, P.J. picked up his backpack and put it on his lap. He slowly and gently unzipped the top a few inches, and was instantly slapped with an apple pie smell that was so strong that it would make any grandmother reminisce. The odor was so pungent that P.J. violently shook his head back and forth, trying to dispel it from his nostrils. No luck. *Too much of a good thing,* P.J. thought.

Thru the darkness of the slight opening of the bag, he saw two eyes looking up at him. It reminded P.J. of his puppy, Riley, when he had done something wrong but still wanted to look cute and innocent. Pinch's little cupped hand was meekly waving. P.J. had a shock of panic. He look left and right quickly. He realized that he was the only student left in the room. Relief started to settle in until Mr. Baldo asked, "Everything okay, P.J.?"

"Sure -- no problem," P.J. replied.

Surely everyone else had noticed. But I guess not, P.J. thought, as he looked at Mr. Baldo gathering his papers and filling his brief-case. Not to push his luck, P.J. flung his backpack onto his right shoulder and slithered out into the hallways of chaos.

P.J. saw Liam ahead in the highway of students heading towards him. "Liam! Liam!"

Liam yelled back in acknowledgement, "P.J.! P.J.!", over the raging river of noise that took over the hallways every hour on the hour. Realizing that they would get swept past each other, P.J. instructed, "Boys Bathroom! Now!"

Liam nodded and started pushing his way sideways cross stream just praying to get to the other side. P.J. stopped dead in his tracks then headed in the same direction. He was first to get there. He opened the door then reached out to drag Liam inside. Once inside, it felt like they were in the eye of a storm.

Two block-shaped jocks, Smash and Ziplock, were show-ing one last flex of their pumped-up bicep muscles in front of the bank of mirrors. As they passed by leaving, the jocks each bumped shoulders with P.J. and Liam, treating them like turn-stiles. These muscle-bound, everyday thugs were just acting like the school bullies that they were. The only good thing is that they left the boys alone to talk.

Liam looked quickly under the stall doors for feet. Both blurted at once trying to talk. Then Liam continued, "Me, first". He set his backpack down on the floor against the wall right next to P.J.'s.

"Dollop's in my backpack. I was sitting in class when I see this hand whacking away at *Monica's* ponytail in front of me. Luckily, she thought it was me."

P.J. interrupted, "Isn't that the girl that you like?"

"Well, yeah, but didn't you hear me? I said Dollop came to school with me. Why aren't you freaking out?!"

P.J. replied, "'Cause guess who's in my backpack? I didn't even know myself until Pinch started farting and snickering in my science class. I guess the smell of the chemicals cooking caused Pinch to think someone else farting so he couldn't help himself. Luckily the bell rang. By the way, don't go into that science lab for a long while, until the strong odor of apple pie seeps out. I used to like that smell."

Just then, they both turned toward the bathroom stalls as the sound of spinning toilet paper rolls started spinning...and spinning... and spinning. Liam and P.J. looked under different stall doors to see the floor around the toilets filling fast with unraveling toilet paper.

Liam whispered hard to P.J., "Who's in there?"

"I thought there was no-one here with us?", P.J. said, perplexed.

Then it stopped, just a suddenly, with the sound of the empty roll rattled frantically on its holder.

Two stall doors opened slowly, like in a scary movie. Then out shuffled two small critters smothered in unraveled toilet paper with the toilet paper rolls placed over their arms and legs. They were like a dwarf combination of a poorly made mummy and a cheap cardboard robot. The robot mummies made groans and stretched out their arms forward. Pinch and Dollop grunted together, "We have come to conquer your world."

After six steps, each tipped over in laughter, falling into their own soft bed of toilet tissue. Dollop turned to Pinch looked at a toilet paper roll and said, "These will be great for "fire flyby" telescopes."

P.J. and Liam snickered in quiet laughter at their two new friends.. Then the bathroom entrance door creaked opened. P.J. and Liam promptly stood at the sinks and pretended to wash their hands. Pinch and Dollop disappeared into the stalls without a word.

Mr. Stronoffski, the school's Assistant Principal and Chief Rules Enforcer, pushed the door open only to be greeted by two smiling, completely-petrified young men scrubbing and drying their hands. They casually picked up their backpacks while looking back to see their smidgeons. They almost made it the door when, Mr. Stronoffski barked, "Stop! Who did this?"

P.J. tried to shuffle Liam out the door as he said without thinking, "I think it was ahhhh... Smash and Ziplock. Gotta go". He knew he was going to pay for that. But at least he had made it out alive and without detention.

Mr. Stronoffski pointed and ordered, "Before you go, you two pick all this toilet paper and cardboard up...now."

He proceeded to wash his hands as the boys slinked back in, scooped up armfuls of toilet paper and shoved it all into the two tall, silo-shaped trash cans near the entrance. Mr. S then continued to watch them suspiciously as he left the bathroom. Both of boys were squishing their last armful of toilet paper into the trash can when Liam asked, "Where'd they go?"

"These guys are incredible at getting lost and hiding. I'm sure, they'll show up.", P.J. answered. As the boys picked up and zipped up their backpacks, they were stopped by a smothered mumbling coming from each of the trash cans. Like synchronized swimmers, Pinch and Dollop popped out of each of the cans like they were whales breaching out of deep water. Gasping for air, they called out, "Here we are!"

Pinch picked some strands of paper from his mouth, while Dollop had a clump sticking out of his left ear. P.J. instructed, "Both of you guys need to get back into our backpacks and stop getting us in trouble...at least until we get home."

The pranksters slumped into their backpack homes while still picking off random strips of tiles paper from their clothes. They zipped themselves up from the inside. Liam flung his backpack over his shoulder and turned to PJ, saying, "You have to admit, they are cool to have around, though." Begrudgingly, P.J. muttered , "True." The two of them slipped back into the hallway and the normal insanity of their day.

P.J. entered his Math class. He sat down, took out the notebook that was handed to him by two little helpful furry hands and proceeded to stare straight ahead, without realizing that he was even doing it. "P.J., P.J., PJ!" called Mr. Dalton. "Are you here today?".

P.J. shook his head vigorously to shake away the cobwebs of the day. He blurted, "Yes, Mr. D."

"Are you feeling Okay?"

"Yes, sir," P.J. said softly.

"Okay, then, what's the answer to the problem on the blackboard?"

P.J. looked up to see the board entirely filled with one gigantic math problem. How long had he been daydreaming? *Crap!*, he thought.

"Well, P.J., What's the answer?"

P.J. started speed-reading the problem on the board, with a momentary break to look to his friends in the class for clues.

Each one shot back a blank look but no help. Mr. Dalton walked to the board and began slowly reviewing the problem from the beginning.

Then a small tug on P.J.'s pant leg broke his temporary panic. It was Pinch. A stubby arm reached out from the backpack, holding a slip of paper with scribbled numbers on it. P.J. took it and promptly ignored it.

Mr. Dalton then turned back to the class. "Anyone else then? ... Anyone?" The students started shooting glances back and forth, as if hoping the answer would appear by magic.

Mr. Dalton then said, "Okay, I'll make a deal with you. If anyone gives me the answer to this problem before the class bell rings, I will treat the entire class to sundaes tomorrow."

Now, that got their attention. Every pencil, pen and broken crayon feverishly started moving in an effort to calculate the answer. The huge black and white clock on the wall showed that there were just seconds to go. Answers, or more like guesses, started flying from around the room: "14!" "48!" "42!"

With seven seconds left, P.J. uncrumpled the piece of paper clutched in his hand, read it outloud, "378!?"

Mr. Dalton looked shocked. After a couple more seconds, he regained his composure and said, "Well looks like P.J. just earned each of you guys an ice cream sundae tomorrow. Good job!"

The school bell rang and a cheer went up as the students head toward the door. P.J. looked down at the peering eyes through the open zipper of his backpack. Pinch's arm reached out and P.J. gave him a high five, way down low. Pinch winked at him and zipped the bag from the inside. P.J. went off to lunch a proud yet confused boy. How could Pinch know the right answer? P.J. was soon sucked up into the abyss of the hallways. All he could hear is his own hungry, gurgling stomach. Now on to the cafeteria for lunch.

P.J., Liam and half the student body lined up, like expressionless prisoners, with plastic trays which they scooted across a waist-high metal bar shelf in front of sterile metal containers. Each metal container was systematically organized seemingly by food color. The interesting thing was that the colors were not any of those seen in nature. The processed "meats" sported a lovely burnt orange-brown from the deep-frying process. All meats and french fries were deep-fried in the same oil, giving any meat of choice the same exact taste as any other. From there, the colors varied. There were the string beans and corn that have had the natural color boiled out of them, just to have it added artificially later. The only item sporting a somewhat natural color was the sheet of brownies, which come from giant bags of brown powder. It always reminded P.J. of the scene in *Oliver Twist* where Oliver asks for more gruel. They slid the trays, lifted their plates, and pointed at the color of choice, which was promptly slopped onto their plate with the same enthusiasm that it was made. Even though it only cost $1.50 total, to P.J. it still seemed like a rip-off.

Then they took their tasteless, colorless trays to their tables. P.J. had always thought of the cafeteria as like a small town with different groups or families, all with their own personalities, at separate tables. There were the jocks, the computer kids, the brainiacs and P.J.'s particular group, which was made up of mixed personalities who have always been friends, no matter what the grade. The coolest or toughest kids had the best positioning at their tables --some near the food line, others near the windows. The brainiacs were near the restrooms. The computer kids near the most electrical outlets. P.J. and Liam's group sat at separate but abutting tables on the edge, near the windows. That kept them out of range of any potential battle...or so they thought.

The moment the boys sat down, P.J. and Liam were answering an onslaught of questions about what had happened in their neighborhood yesterday. Their stories got longer and more descriptive as time went on, but basically stayed truthful. On the way back from the food line, Smash, Ziplock and a few of their gorilla-like posse stopped right in front of P.J. at his table. They mumbled to each of their previous conquests and humiliations, saying things like, "Remember when we stuck that twerp's head in the toilet and flushed?".

Smash stopped and stared at P.J. He was mad. "Mr. S. gave me detention for the mess that you made in the men's room," he declared. "He said that you and your brother blamed me. I don't appreciate people lying about me. You're gonna pay for it."

The cafeteria went silent. P.J. tried to mutter out some sort of excuse and explanation. It never came out. Smash turned and led his bunch of thought-less baboons back to their table. P.J. and Liam realized that the end of their lives as they knew them was over. It's that dilemma of knowing you are going to die, but not when. *Well at least I know it's soon*, thought P.J.

As the parade of thugs walked away, a scoop of mashed potatoes flew through the air, landing on Smash's back just below his neck. It stuck there for a moment and then, like a snail leaving a slime trail, started to slither down his back.

P.J.'s eyes felt like they were going to pop out of his head, while Liam squished down in his seat to make a smaller target yet giggled quietly into his sleeve. Smash barely noticed, but his cohorts certainly knew. Smash whipped around to face the boys and said, "Did you do that?"

Both brothers honestly answered. "No." Liam added, "...Sir".

Smash and his crew scanned the crowd, now all staring directly at them. Not knowing exactly where the attack had come from, the gang gave P.J. and Liam one last glare, then turned away again.

They had barely taken three steps when two clumps of mashed potatoes flew through the air. One splatted on the back of Smash's head. The other soared at Ziplock, and, when he turned to see, it slapped him right between the eyes.

P.J. looked innocently in return, until he looked down to see fingerprints from wet mashed potatoes around the zipper of his backpack on the floor.

The future felons turned in unison with their trays, ready to throw them at P.J. and Liam's tables. This triggered the kids at P.J. and Liam's tables to stand up and yell, "FOOD FIGHT!!!!" They all threw their trays of slop at the charging wall of fury (the bullies).

The thug army stopped dead in their tracks, as from every direction the cafeteria food was flying and landing on top of them. Bombs of tater tots, chicken nuggets, mashed potatoes, grayish green beans—all landing directly on top of them. It couldn't have been executed better. On display right in front of P.J. and Liam's table stood a humiliated band of bullies, drenched in dripping food.

Smash and his conspirators began to wipe sludge from their eyes and ears. Smash even scooped out a concoction of goo that was heading down his back into his underwear. If there was ever a ball of pure hatred, this was it. They stood drowning in waves of snickers and laughter. They were stunned. They were frozen in anger. Then slowly, they began to step forward towards P.J. and Liam, like mummies walking for the first time in a thousand years.

Just as they were taking their second step, two large squirrels darted out of nowhere. They soared towards the bullies from the edge of the cafe tables and landed directly on Smash and Ziplock.

As if planned, these two blurs of fur zipped to top of the bullies' heads, under their crotches, and even down their pants legs. These uncoordinated mounds of muscle danced and twitched in the center of the cafeteria. The invading squirrels only stopped occasionally to taste a sampling of the sloppy seconds of food and then spit it out, to acknowledge that it was disgusting even to them. The entire cafeteria leapt back, leaving the gang all alone in the center. The onlookers broke into side-splitting laughter. Many of the spectators took out their phones and began filming this once-in-a-lifetime moment. These two seemingly-rabid squirrels zipped so fast that these "previously-seen-as-bad" boys thought they were surrounded by hundreds of them. Looking for some way to escape, they foolishly climbed on top of one of the center tables and to better swat at these furry flurries. The squirrels were so fast that it looked like the bullies were jerking around and hitting themselves on purpose for no good reason. Smash began to try to curl up into a ball while still standing. Then Ziplock and the others tried to smack the squirrels away from each other. Smash, Ziplock and the brotherhood of evil squeaked and squealed over and over, like they were little frightened kids. The cameras got closer as the whimpering grew louder. Just as it reached a fever pitch, the squirrels were gone.

Bursting through the cafeteria doors came Mr. S., who slowly approached the nervous-twitching masses of shame standing the table. He folded his arms and said, "What are you boys doing up there on the table!?"

Mr. S. took the beaten souls away to the principal's office in shame. The bullies pointed adamantly at P.J. and Liam and said, "IT WAS THEM!". The brothers just kept quiet as Mr. S. said, "Those two young men have already cleaned up one of your messes. This time, it's your turn."

"But they sicced squirrels on us!", Smash blurted. "They were vicious and were going to kill us."

Mr. S turned to little doe-eyed Deirdre and asked, "Do you know what they're talking about? Did you see squirrels?"

She looked over at Liam, winked, and said, "I have no idea what they are talking about."

The rest of the students joined in. Squirrels? They must be crazy.

Mr. S. herded the bullies out while the whole cafeteria broke into cheers...even the football coach joined in. The era of terror had finally ended.

The mob was soon dispersed by other teachers who arrived. The teachers were slipping and half-sliding on food puddles, while the students high-fived each other and compared videos and photos on their phones. It was already on the Internet and soon become folklore in their little town. P.J. and Liam were treated like royalty school-wide now. Everyone just assumed that P.J. and Liam orchestrated this yet P.J. knew differently.

The rest of the day was blur as people patted the boys on the back, thanking them vigorously in the hallway, or even random intense hugs from all of those who had been previously humiliated by Smash and his gang.

In just a few days, a local rapper, Nutty D, made a video with footage of Smash and his gang dancing and squealing on the cafe tables in a dance song called "Squirrel Dance (I see squirrels)." Even though the squirrels were moving so fast that you don't even see them, it went viral. It was a "Smash" hit.

Life is good, thought P.J.

THREE

Going Home

"**H**oney!", shouted P.J. and Liam's Dad as he swung the boys' bedroom door open to see piles of clothes, video games and empty candy wrappers, but no boys, "Have you seen the boys?"

Mom yelled back, "They must have gone out with their friends. It IS Saturday morning."

"I guess", he muttered to himself with a quick sniff. "Dear, do we have any apple pie?" Descending the stairs, he continued, "Boy, they were acting strange last night. They were acting, using strange voices and moving stuff around all night. After all that, I would have thought that they would be exhausted and sleep in."

Only half-listening, Mom said, "Get your stuff — we have to go. They'll be fine. They came straight in from school last night, shut their door tight and then they played all night. They're responsible - like you." Still a little perplexed, he muttered "And a little crazy, like you." She heard it, though. "Hey!" she said, and accentuated it with a light slap on his butt on the way out the door.

"We should have told Mom," Liam said, while adjusting the backpack over his shoulder.

P.J. asked, "What were you planning on telling her?"

"Well, hmmmm."

"Exactly", P.J. said, "This way we don't lie."

Liam nodded, even though he knew it wasn't quite right.

They both knew that the Smidgeons had to go home...to their home. Liam was just too excited to see where the Smidgeons lived. The journey of these four fast friends began with the incessant barking of their lovable lab, Riley, who followed happily until stopped by his yard leash (which has broken from in the past). They trudged through the backyard, past the pool, past the tree house, through the woods and finally to a spot far enough away from the house that the only things that looked familiar were the old Christmas trees that their Dad would leave there every January for the local birds and wildlife to use. P.J. and Liam, along with their new friends shimmied and partially slid down a leaf-covered hill to the bottom. The chorus of Riley's frustrated yelps slowly faded as they worked their way farther from home.

P.J. asked, "What's eating at him?"

Liam answered, "He's just jealous. He wants to come with us."

Down at the bottom of the hill, the boys were ready to continue their journey by walking off into the woods, but Dollop was standing before three cut, dried pine trees fashioned into an upside down triangle. It had been placed at the base of an ancient oak with exposed roots that stretched out from the exposed slope like the fingers of an old woman holding an imaginary ball. Dollop reached out and parted two of the trees to reveal a large hole at the base of a great oak tree.

The opening was only three feet high. Pinch held the tree doors open and looked back. Dollop just walked straight in, leaving P.J.

and Liam standing there dumbfounded. They thought, *What was happening? How could this all be so close to their home without them ever knowing?*

Pinch looked back and said to them, "Come on, I can't stand here all day."

As they approached, Dollop quickly realized the size issue. He had never really considered that his new friends would be too tall for the entrance. P.J. slowly began to step forward, trying to size up how his tall lanky body would possibly fit. Liam, on the other hand, just pushed P.J. aside and dropped to his hands and knees. He was not going to miss this. All of his life, he had felt small compared to his older brother, but no longer. He felt like a giant adventurer. This was his time to lead the way.

P.J. fell to his knees and shuffled, like a timid dog into the dirt cave entrance. P.J. banged his head immediately on the edge of the mossy entrance while he was busy trying to look around. Liam, on the other hand, was far ahead of P.J. and just behind Pinch. Pinch being the good host occasionally checked behind him to verify that Liam was still keeping up. The walls of the tunnel suddenly transformed from the packed earth with tiny bare plant roots hanging from the ceiling to a smooth, hard surface. Liam wanted to investigate closer but was just too afraid to slow down and lose sight of his tour guide, Pinch. Light brown, slightly curved tiles now covered the entire tunnel walls, floor and ceiling. *The craftsmanship was just beautiful,* P.J. thought. He could tell that each one was delicately placed by hand and cared for regularly.

Liam was far enough down the tunnel to no longer see any light from the world above. Liam stopped briefly and sniffed the air, just like his dog, Riley would, when supper was being served. Liam then asked, "Why does it smell like peanut butter?"

Pinch kept on walking not breaking his stride, until he stopped abruptly in front of an open doorway to his left. Liam stopped crawling to catch his breath only to go speechless as he looked into the first of many massive rooms filled with nuts (acorns to be more exact). Pinch proudly started to explain, "You see... for generations, when my friends go to your world, they appear to be squirrels. To look like real squirrels, they have to...."

Liam interrupted, "They carry back acorns," as if answering a trivia game.

"Actually," Pinch continued, "they bring them back into the tunnel and discard them into a room like this. We use them for everything from the tiling on the walls throughout our whole unground world to special treats that you'll probably see later."

This tour stop gave P.J. enough time to join them. Catching his breath (as much as you can on all fours in a giant worm hole underground), P.J. was confused by the opening on the left with heaping mini-mountains of acorns. "Cool", was all he said though. P.J. then turned and asked, "What do you do with all of those?"

Pinch, always the gracious host, answered, " We use them for what we call "peanut butter", tiles for our walls...", as he pointed to the tiny, tan shell tiles which encircled them, "abrasives for cleaning, and just about everything that you build with human cement or plastic."

Then P.J. said quietly to himself, "We are down underground in the dark, probably hundreds of feet, but there is still light."

Pinch reached out and inserted his right arm into an eye-level (for him anyway) hole in the wall and pulled a glass jar filled with fireflies. They danced in the air in circles inside the jar even though there was no cover to keep them in.

Pinch explained, "Fireflies are like your honey bees. You see, fireflies live underground for the first winter of their lives. These are like firefly nurseries. They like the darkness and actually like lighting up their surroundings. As you can tell, it's nice and dark down here. We just put fresh leaves in the bottom of the jars, and the fireflies come in when they are hungry. Did you know that they are actually beetles, and, depending on where they live, they have different colors. They light themselves up to find each other in the dark. That same light also helps light our tunnels so we can get back and forth from the world above."

Dollop anxiously waved his right arm forward, telling Liam, "Come on, we can't stay here all day."

Pinch started to walk, almost run when he tripped and fell face first, with his arms outstretched in front of him on the nut tiled floor. He stood up, annoyed, and looked back to see what had tripped him. Pinch looked back to Liam as if to ask without words, "Do you see that?"

In the dim light, P.J. saw a groggy Smidgeon complete with acorn shell shield and a wooden spear. The startled young warrior stood slowly, squinting trying to see if he was still dreaming. The scruffy voice snorted softly, "Pinch, is that you?" somewhere between afraid and confused.

"Tidbit?", answered Pinch. "Tidbit, what are you doing here?"

Tidbit lowered his ornate wooden spear and said, sheepishly, "I played one too many practical jokes on my brother, and the elders sent me here to guard the entrance and well you know....". Now looking down at his feet in shame, he continued, "I got bored here and fell asleep. You're not going to tell, are you?"

Before Pinch could answer, Liam politely introduced himself "Hi, I'm Liam." With that, Tidbit sprung back into a fierce warrior pose, with spear pointed towards the danger (namely Liam) and looked deep into the eyes of a human. In the blink of an eye, Liam's friendly outstretched hand was next to a seemingly empty crumpled acorn vest and spear. Liam pulled back slightly. He began to wonder if he had some sort of magical power when wiggling started under the pile of armor. Liam looked to Pinch to see if he did something wrong. Pinch look assuredly back. Just then a brownish-grey wet nose poked through the armor arm opening and after one last look back at Liam, scurried (as squirrels do) off down the hallway.

"Well, they'll know we're coming now," Pinch knowingly snipped. Dollop asked from the deep dim-lit tunnel, "Who was that?", wondering what the hold-up was.

Pinch answered, "It was Tidbit, Sir". Pinch just looked amused snapping back to treating Dollop like the royalty that he was.

Tidbit shot down the main hallway without his armor on, like a spear from a mighty Smidgeon warrior, to announce that Pinch and Dollop had returned, and with two human prisoners, as well. "There's three ways to spread the word in my world", Pinch told Liam," Tele-phone. Tele-gram. Tell- Tidbit."

Turning back and talking over his shoulder, Pinch continued, "Sir, we better walk a little faster before Tidbit starts telling them that we are being invaded by armies of humans and he fought them off." Dollop nodded slightly and agreed. "Let's Go."

Just when Liam and PJ's knees and hunched backs were starting to get sore, they noticed the ceiling of their gigantic shell-covered gopher hole was rising. Finally, Liam and P.J. could start to stand slowly and stretch. Ahead was a set of doors so large that you could drive their school bus through them. P.J., who was awestruck, asked, "How in the world did they...I mean you...build such a beautiful structure like this, all under our world."

The doors were made of what looked like wood. But they sparkled. Upon closer inspection, P.J. and Liam stood face to face with this magnificent architecture. They first noticed that the wooden doors were actually a remanufactured nut shell made to look like wood that was carved in one piece from the area's largest oak tree.

The sparkles were alive. Literally alive. The doors were polished with a shiny, hard, clear coating that attracted fireflies to land, light up in happiness and taste the coating, like a honey bee eating from the belly of a delicious flower. P.J. and Liam felt humbled and amazed examining every fine detail. This alone was worth the trip. P.J. reached out to touch the wall of fireflies and they moved. It was as if his hand repelled them. His clammy palm touched the bare semi-sticky wall of the door. "Cooool," he exclaimed. After a moment of two, a smaller door swung open at Dollop's eye level with two eyes peering outward from the center.

"Who goes there, and what are your intentions?!", asked a deep, menacing voice that seemed born for the role. Pinch walked up to the one-foot square door like he was stepping up to place his order at the human's favorite take-out place. He declared, "This is Pinch and a few of my friends, just let me in." Almost apologetically he answered softly, "It's not you, it's them" as he looked past Pinch at the human boys.

Dollop then stepped forward, not being accustomed to this type of hesitation, and said, "Is there a problem, Bantam? Just open the door." Stunned silent, the only response was the creaking sound of the opening doors. Pinch and Dollop walked knowingly into the expanding opening while P.J. and Liam stood as if they had just seen Santa Claus in person. They stared in silence and frozen, not knowing what to do next. Dollop directed, "Guys, come on!" through his teeth, as if embarrassed.

P.J. and Liam looked in and up in wonder. "Magnificent", P.J. said to Liam. Liam never heard that word before from P.J. but it seemed to fit. They entered what looked like a grand railroad station, several stories high, with staircases interweaving against the walls. Dozens, maybe even hundreds, of Smidgeons of virtually all shapes, sizes and ages, buzzed to and fro, as if they were in a rush to somewhere. Then a wave swept across the room from left to right as they whispered to one another. They then stopped right where they stood, and just stared. They seemed to stare directly at P.J. and Liam. With one loud series of pops, they instantly transformed into squirrels, a defense mode they adopted when they were being attacked. Once these Smidgeons changed to look like squirrels, they scattered for covered behind doorways, furniture even each other, never letting their eyes leave the sight of these frightful beasts.

Then, just as quickly, one-by-one the squirrel look-alikes dropped down to their front elbows, like show horses bowing to their owners, to honor their lost king's return. The freakishly large (for this room anyway) humans standing behind Dollop just didn't seem to be as interesting, now that their king had returned. Dollop stood regally and looked around with growing pride. He began to wave his hand side to side at the wrist as he caught the eyes of each individual royal subject. Dollop took it all in with one deep breath. They could see in his eyes that he cared about each one of them. And they loved him in return. A second wave washed over the Great Room, consisting of shock, then confusion, pure glee and finally honor for the long-dreamed about return of their never forgotten warrior King. Liam was simply amazed. His head was spinning around, like a kitten watching a butterfly flickering over his head. Liam tapped Dollop on the shoulder, which seem to break the king's spell. Liam asked, "Is that statue over there of you? How about that painting over there?" He was pointing at artwork prominently placed on the palace walls. "Yup...", replied Dollop through his closed toothed smile, "Although I was a little younger and thinner then," he said, patting his slightly bulging stomach. King Dollop waiting for every last smidgeon to stop and kneel. The once-bustling bee-hive of life stood silent. Everything went eerily silent. Just then, The King declared, "I have returned with Pinch, and these two mighty "human" warriors who have made this all possible. Treat them like they are my family. Tonight we celebrate our return!" The responding cheers were almost deafening. Then just as quickly, like the popping of a popcorn kernels, Smidgeons reappeared in their places (no longer afraid). P.J. blurted out with his mouth still wide open from the sight, "This is so cool. Its like having fireworks indoors." Dollop said confidently, " You haven't seen anything, yet."

"Come with me," instructed the king. P.J., Liam and Pinch followed close behind. Their bodies moved forward but their heads continued to whip around like a horned owl in a feeding frenzy. It was like walking into a dream...together.

P.J. thought, *The details are simply incredible. It must have taken them centuries of craftsmanship to create this impressive sight.* The tourist mini-parade marched from the Great Room and entered a hallway to the left. Down this hallway were a series of rooms on both sides. Each room was filled with Smidgeon children, all facing their professor. Dollop, in a quieter voice, turned to his visitors and said calmly, "These are our classrooms. This is our future you see before you." They stopped at one of the doorways and peered in, trying not to be noticed. Not so easy when the boys were so much taller and odder looking than everyone else. Their heads alone seemed half the size of the students.

The professor, whose back was to them, lectured, "When you take the chunk of your rock in your right hand, remember to create a spin that will cause it to arch. This arch fools the fireflies, and will ensure a cleaner strike." Liam squished his face as if he had just eaten something sour. Pinch whispered over his shoulder, "What's wrong?"

Liam said, concerned, "What about the fireflies? I don't like that you hurt the fireflies for sport, that's all."

Pinch continued, a little confused, "No. no. no. If you listen very close you could hear a squeal like the motor of your planes. If you listen even closer, you'll hear that the firefly scream is pure joy. They are squealing "Weeeeee!" They get a thrill out of suddenly spinning in a new direction, like riding a roller coaster for the first time. Remember, fireflies are very important to us. Just like your honey bees. Our lives depend and revolve around theirs."

Liam grinned in relief, "Ohhhh."

Dollop began to walk forward to the next open door on the right. The stodgy professor recited (as if for the thousandth time), "Now to review yet again, written history has our tribes beginning roughly 15,000 years ago spreading from this area throughout the northern regions of the world wherever nuts fall from trees and squirrels live. There are 200 types of squirrels and they live on every continent but Australia and Antartica. The largest are likely the ones in India which grow up to one meter in length. Around here though they are much smaller, of course."

A few of the students who were actually paying attention moved their eyes without ever removing their chins off of their cupped hands to look at the bizarre, peering strangers.

Next, the king's tour walked by a working kitchen with a small sign entitled, "Cooking with Nuts." Liam said to P.J., "I'd like to have that sign on our wall when we try cooking with Dad."

P.J. snorted a laugh, trying to hold it back out of respect. Dollop announced, "They're busy making food for tonight's banquet." Suddenly Liam remembered that he was hungry.

Next up, on the left was Smidgeon Biology. The stuffy professor recited through his teeth, "This transformation into a squirrel look-alike happens when your blood pressure rises over this point. It's nothing to be ashamed of. It's perfectly natural. If does not happen naturally, just stick your thumb in your mouth and blow as hard you can for 10 seconds." Then just as quickly, sporadic popping sounds were followed with studious squirrels sitting upright in their seats.

P.J. said, "That's cool. Its like watching life-sized popcorn pop."

Liam trailed behind a little while he almost passes out while trying to blow out extra hard with his thumb is his mouth. A little fart popped out from Liam. Liam looking around realizing that someone might have actually seen, heard or even smelled him. He hurriedly caught back up to the procession, as if he had never left.

The last school room was the largest. The students all seemed to be smiling and paying attention with pen and paper in hand, writing feverishly. Outside was a scratch and sniff sign announcing, "The History of Practical Jokes." The professor stood seriously before the class with a multicolored hat and extra-long floppy shoes. He declared, "So, in review for the final, we will cover: salt on toothbrushes, the improper uses of Super Glue, food that you lick and put back for others to eat, fake vomit, the art of itching powder, puzzles with one piece missing, switching shoes for smaller sizes, peanut butter on toilet seats and, finally, today's lesson of how to make a fart sound appear to be coming from a friend. To do this, first you need to..."

Dollop lead the visitors' single-file onward before Liam could hear the end of that last statement. Liam muttered, "I wish I could be a Smidgeon."

At the end of the hall, they took a sharp left. This led them to a maze of tunnels laced with carefully crafted wooden doors, each of which was adorned with polished home numbers. Dollop led P.J. and Liam to the end of the longest hall. At the end, they stopped and Dollop opened a door that was much taller and ornate then the others. "You gentleman can rest in here for a little while, while they prepare for our banquet."

Dollop entered and stretched out his arm to welcome them in. "This is only used for visiting dignitaries and honored guests like yourselves. Watch your heads." Just then Liam smacked his forehead on one of the interwoven hanging roots that decorated the ceiling. "Ouch," he squawked, followed by, "No, it was my fault. I was too busy looking around."

This room was filled with the finest of materials, arts and furniture that the Smidgeons had collected and constructed over the centuries. Most of the tables and furniture were sized to fit Smidgeons. P.J. had never felt so freakishly huge as just this moment. It was like they just walked into their little sister's room with play tea sets and tables.

The only exceptions were two extra-large (for smidgeons) royal king size and queen size wooden chairs up against the back wall. Liam stumbled over and promptly sat sloppily like Jell-o in the palm of your hand in the smaller of the two thrones. He draped his limbs over the arm rests and stretched out his legs so awkwardly that he was sure that his mom would yell at him. P.J., on the other hand, gently and regally slid delicately and respectfully in his adjacent throne. He was quickly entranced with the arms of the chair that were carved to resemble a twisted vine, ending with a smooth, rounded lion head. His palms fit so naturally over the scalp of the lion's head. His fingers seemed to trickle into the lion's open mouth. The chair's upholstery material was so smooth and soft that they knew they could fall asleep right there. The throne sturdy legs mimicked the encircled vine arm design. Each of the four legs were anchored with carved lion paws. They looked almost life-sized. Liam lifted his head just enough to say, "I want these for my room."

While they pretended to be resting, the boys scanned the room. They noticed clear glass jars hanging from the ceiling's polished roots with fireflies in full glow. The walls looked like a brownish cement but upon closer inspection, they appeared and smelled like crushed acorn shells. An immense, hollowed out acorn served as a drinking cup. Carved tree slices carved as dishes. The weary travelers soon succumbed to exhaustion right where they sprawled.

After what seemed like just a few moments later, there was a knock on the door, which then opened to admit two Smidgeon soldiers, complete with acorn-shelled armor and ancient helmets, each topped with sparrow feathers in the shape of a squirrel tail. "The King has requested your presence in the Great Room," the soldier on the right said.

The two soldiers stood stiffly and patiently at each side of the door, waiting for the lumbering giants to waken without any prodding.

"Wow. I must have been tired," P.J. mumbled to Liam.

"Me, too", Liam replied as he rubbed the sleep from his eyes. They stood (as well as they could) and brushed themselves off, to look more presentable. Liam, now fully awake, exclaimed, "Time to party."

They all marched obediently in tow down the hallways of what looked like families' apartments, then passed the now-empty school rooms and into the spectacular expanse of the Great Room.

They weaved through groups of younger smidgeons all dressed in their fanciest attire. P.J. and Liam were led to two throne-like chairs on a stage, just like in the room they had left, one on either side of King Dollop's throne. There were stained and polished pine wood banquet tables hand-crafted from the pine trees that were left mysteriously by their kingdom entrance every year, deep in the heart of winter. Three rows of tables stretched from one end of the room to the other.

At the far end, there sat Dollop. P.J., wondering whether he should be bowing or not, said, "You look impressive...your majesty."

The King was draped in the finest clothing made of plush royal burgundy satin with polished gold buttons, with glittering jewelry from all around the world, all topped with a crown that the Queen of England would envy. Grasped in his left hand was a golden scepter. The base appeared to be made of interwoven lustrous tree roots, similar to those that they had seen on the chairs in their guest room. Sparkling rubies dotted the luminous shaft and at the pinnacle was a life-sized crystal glass acorn. King Dollop, began waving it around for emphasis while he talked, remarked to the boys, "They like it when I wear all of this for fancy occasions." Scratching under his left armpit, he continued, "It's a little itchy sometimes, but it could be worse." Then, he stood and in his best "royal", deep voice he declared, "Let's the festivities begin!"

Blusterous horns trumpeted from walkways above the walls. Twelve royal guardsmen, adorned in bright, larger than life colors marched down the aisles. In an informal parade of enthusiasm following them, bounced and bopped a swarm of young, energetic smidgeons dressed as fairy-like fireflies. Each costume was light, airy and physically sparkled. The costumes actually lit up the more that they gyrated and danced. Dollop pointed with his scepter towards them, then, slightly embarrassed, said to Liam, "I used to have to dress up like that."

Liam smirked and replied, "I like what you have now much better."

"Me, too," the king retorted. The guardsmen then split into two lines at the stage front and left the bouncing fireflies to dance and prance in one bubbling mass of energy. The king said to his guests, "You two can choose this year's Prince and Princess of the Fireflies. Liam, you choose the prince. P.J., you choose the princess. Choose whichever ones that you feel best demonstrate the spirit of fireflies." The partially befuddled boys noticed that he wasn't kidding and proceeded to study the glowing ball of confusion, each looking for that special one.

Liam was first. "I like that boy." Liam pointed at a rough and tumble boy who was bumping into other "fireflies" with his eyes closed. "He's trying so hard and reminds me of a pinball machine—when he bumps into the others, they all light up."

P.J.'s concentration was so intense, he was biting his lower lip. P.J. finally pointed at the smallest young lady, in lime green lace, who was dancing carefully on her tiptoes with her hands holding up both sides of her handmade lace dress like a ballerina when she curtsied. "She's perfect."

With that, Pinch arrived from the side and singled out the two winners. They were so busy performing that they barely noticed him at first. Pinch herded the the gaggle of dancing "fireflies" up to the stage and turned the two delighted winners towards the crowd. Pinch stood behind them and exclaimed, "We have our winners!"

The applause was almost deafening, coming even from those "fireflies" who weren't picked. Stiff guardsmen came in from the wings with the winners' crowns. They looked at first glance like ordinary crowns, but soon you could see that the top piece was clear hand-blown glass and inside were flickering fireflies in full light. The two were both visibly shaking from the excitement as King Dollop placed the crowns on the heads. He stood tall, proud and puffed out his chest and bellowed, "I give you our new Firefly Prince and Princess!"

King Dollop then returned to his throne as the winners edged their way to their families through thunderous applause and congrats pats on the back. There was so much excitement and jostling, the prince and princess had to secure the crowns with both hands to their head. The newly crowned Princess could barely see through the crown brim that was so big that it wanted to slip over her eyes. To her, it was just the right size. Then, two dozen trumpeters, each with a drummer to their left all rose on a stage to the right of the king's royal platform.

With a sudden jerk, the stage lurched to the perfect height for everyone in the ballroom to look up to them. Every eye in the place, Smidgeons and humans alike, gazed in wonder and expectation. Then the lead drummer chanted "One. Two..." as the drummers raised their sticks in an "X" far above their heads and the trumpeters raised their horns to their lips. Complete silence. Then he shouted "Three!" The band began with a jolt, playing a dance tune that was so infectious, the entire room swayed up and down with every note. P.J. and Liam gazed in delight over the flowing, bobbing waves of ecstatic bubbles of excitement. The boys tried to jump up too, anticipating when the waves would reach them at their peak, like when they would when they would go to the beach.

Ripples turned into waves and waves crashed into each other to the rhythm of the pulsating music. The beats pulsed through them making them forget at the moment that they are underground surrounded by gyrating Smidgeons. Then as if on cue, in the clearing center stood the prince and princess and snaking behind them. One by one added their uncles, aunts, cousins, then came their friends and neighbors. Then came *their* friends and neighbors, until the entire line was connected with their hands to the hips of the one in front of them into one continuously slithering snake of dancers. It looked like that dance that Liam saw at his aunt's wedding. Not knowing what to do in this case, P.J. and Liam just stood still, as everyone there knew exactly what to do but them. Then without warning, Dollop swooped by their sides and grabbed their hands and connected them into the enormous disco caterpillar line even they were just so much bigger. Before they knew it, the giant human brothers were trying their best, swaying and kicking to the side with every beat. Then...

BOOOM!

A shock wave shook the entire room in one mean shake to the left. The music kept trying to go on. The dance line fractured in many areas with bejeweled Smidgeons falling like domino pieces on a shaken table. P.J. and Liam looked at each bewildered yet tried to keep dancing to the pulsing beat by looking at the feet of those in front of them but noticing many of their fellow dancers stumbled to the ground. Then...

BOOOM!

The entire room itself shook again to the right. Scattered fallen pieces of the dancing caterpillar started to think about getting back into line yet again when there came a piercing chorus of shrill high-pitched warning whistles came from the sentry soldiers on the floor near the great doors. With that sound, the remaining bopping band members stopped. Every dancer in line stopped. Every waiter stopped. All the Smidgeons were frozen in place, still as statues, for three full seconds.

Then, just as suddenly, everyone scrambled with a second blast of warning whistles. No one panicked. It was as if they were doing something that had been rehearsed a thousand times before. Mothers and children huddled and walked briskly to their homes and closed doors behind them. Younger Smidgeon teenagers manned the stock room doors and began passing out intricately ornate armor, which the Smidgeon adults promptly buckled and secure onto their bodies, as if preparing for attack. One younger

Smidgeon scooped something that looked like peanut butter from a nearby barrel. He handed a scoop to each soldier after his armor was on. The warriors then stuffed the gooey glob into each hairy ear to muffle the alarm sound. Once all of them were fully suited, they self-organized into precisely squared blocks of soldiers in the center of the grand ballroom facing the visitor entrance.

While this all was happening, P.J. and Liam stood perfectly still with their hands covering their ears against the painfully squealing alarm. Dollop scooted up to them with some of the paste, which they promptly stuffed into their own ears. The boys hunched over looked down and did as they were told. Then Dollop quickly guided them to the rear wall of the room. Their friend, Dollop then mouthed to the boys, "Stand here! You'll be fine."

Liam asked with his lips and his hands, "What's going on?"

Dollop replied animatedly with his hands too, "We have an unwelcome visitor. Don't worry we'll protect you."

P.J. and Liam looked at each other and then at the new defensive military presence. They heard through their ear goop a slightly terrifying, almost deafening rumbling and snorting echoing from the visitors' entrance to their left. *What could this be? What would this creature want so badly that it would crawl down this far under the earth? Was it a rapid badger on a rampage to take over the entire world by enslaving the Smidgeon race? Maybe...*

BOOOM!

Three Smidgeon warrior guardsmen fled away from the visitor entrance doors screaming in an unrecognizable high pitch. Each soared by the band of warriors and ran right to the back of the hall and begin pounding on the doors of their family homes, screeching "Let me in! Let me in! It's coming!" This didn't look good.

The rumbling stopped in a collective gasp as the two elephant-sized ancient wooden doors burst open at once. The most ferocious pair of wide-open jaws smashed their way in from the tunnel opening. Saliva dripped from this monster's ominous sharp teeth. Dozens of fearless (somewhat) Smidgeon soldiers stood firm in block groups with wooden spears pointed high in the belly of the grand room. As the massive furry, dragon-like creature filled the rear portion of the ballroom, it stopped in place and shook. Saliva-soaked mud, dust and chunks of the custom entrance walls flew everywhere—onto the soldiers, the ceiling and even P.J. and Liam who started to poke around the corner to see for themselves. A Smidgeon soldier (with an oversized armor of peanut shells) was uncontrollably vomiting as he tried to wipe off the mucous-like slime that dripped onto his face from the once pristine, sparkling chandelier hanging above. He quivered uncontrollably, flicking giant wads of saliva from his eyes and ears as he dared never look up again...ever. This once fearless soldier now remained curled up under the edge of one of the banquet tables. He watched dozens of soldiers legs buzz passed by and around him as if once in a hornets nest that was just smashed with a baseball bat. The steady bands of soldiers in the center of the grand ballroom lifted their shields as one with every deafening roar and spray of fresh, sticky (maybe poisonous) globs of saliva that was quickly coating there once magnificent shields. Grandmothers shuffled the last strangler youngsters with their large, black cloth cloaks, which absorbed every sloppy drop of slime that reached the back of the room.

The only ones standing remarkably still and almost unshaken were P.J., Liam and a very confused Dollop. One regal warrior stood fearlessly out in front of the boys, while he kept looking up into their eyes to see embarrassment, not fear. Dollop was impressed, and yet still confused.

A befuddled amusement raced across the boys' faces as they

finally looked up at the creature and now recognized this ferocious monster. Liam lifted two fingers to his lips and whistled. A
piercing whistle stopped the chaos at least long enough for him to
yell, "Riley! Sit!"

The seemingly deadly creature sat down with head up and
tongue heavily panting from the side of his mouth right where
he sat on the edge of the grand ballroom. Every Smidgeon in the
stunned room stopped and looked on in awe. No one moved a
muscle, except Liam, who turned to Dollop. "Your Majesty, can
you have some of your soldiers roll eight wooden barrels full of
that peanut butter stuff to directly in front of the beast?" Without
hesitation, Dollop gave hand signals to some of his elite warriors
and they proceeded to roll the barrels directly in front of the hulk-
ing creature that nearly filled one corner of the Great Room now.
The barrels stood tall at the feet of the giant. Few Smidgeons hav-
en't seen many humans let alone "outside world" dogs and never
ones inside their home.

Liam instructed, "Now have them open the tops of the barrels
and back away." As they did as they were told, the monster's drool
dripping increased until it became a disgusting gelatinous stream
of goo coming from its lips puddling on the floor around its feet.
The soldiers carefully backed away with big, long steps, expecting
to run at any moment.

Once clear, Liam shouted, "Riley, Peanut Butter! Good Boy!"
Riley's massive, sand-paper textured, saliva covered tongue
stretched out into each barrel and devoured every morsel...one
by one.

"Your Majesty, now could you have your men place more barrels all of the way down the tunnel and out in the woods to the
back yard of our house?" The cautious yet relieved soldiers rolled
barrel upon barrel out the tunnel as instructed,

The moment they were finished, Riley looked up from his treat with traces still on his outstretched whiskers. Liam sternly yelled, "Riley! Peanut Butter! Go!" as he pointed forcefully to the tunnel. Riley, without even thinking, spun around and squished back into the tunnel. His massive tail wagged happily back and forth, sending banquet furnishings flying like a tropical hurricane whipping around straw trees. The horde of still stunned soldiers began to chuckle and elbow each other with big butt jokes, since all they could see was the dog's furry backside scooting out the tunnel.

Dollop turned to Liam and said, "Thank you. Where can I learn that trick?"

"I can teach you, it's easy if you have enough peanut butter or acorn butter anyway," Liam replied.

"That we have," the King proclaimed, as he waved his arms to show off the nut shell-covered walls.

Then with one final thrust into the tunnel came a blast of gas --a fart that instantly filled the entire underground, closed-in area. P.J. and Liam chuckled as they held their shirt sleeves over their noses. P.J. muttered, "Riley's farts don't smell like apple pie, do they?"

Liam chuckled and remarked, "I didn't think about this possibility with him blocking the only fresh air source we have."

P.J. added, "It kind of smells like yours," trying to joke with his little brother.

Liam positioned his nose in the air as if sniffing a fancy flower and answered, "I guess it does." Meanwhile, they looked around and saw Smidgeons picking up broken banquet pieces with one hand and covering their noses from the stench with napkins in the other. The small soldier still partially covered in slime under the banquet table tried desperately to hold his breath. His cheeks were full with air until he just couldn't hold it anymore. He would burst like an untied balloon and then have to breath in a huge breath and smell of noxious fumes. It was so disgusting for him that, after he get a full breath, his entire body would shiver as if it was trying to instantly get rid it.

They were all prepared to stand in agony with this ghastly stench. Then Liam said, "I have an idea."

With a hand over his face still, Liam walked over to the young soldier in such misery, bent down, and tickled him. At first, he tickled gently and politely, then harder and more aggressively. The young smidgeon couldn't contain himself and farted.

"I'm gonna fight fire with fire!", Liam yelled to P.J. and the King. P.J. caught on to the idea right away and grabbed the nearest Smidgeon and started tickling. P.J. dug and twisted his fingers into his side. In no time, one after one soldiers farted...alot. King Dollop now understood what Liam was trying to do and yelled in his most demanding voice, "Everyone tickle!" Little by little, the vile stench of Riley's toxic fart was replaced by the strangely reassuring odor of apple pie. After a while, the dog fart smell was completely replaced. On the floor sprawled overturned Smidgeons in uniform, squirming and flailing in laughter like flipped-over bugs that have gone completely crazy. Then a few moments later, they all lay with backs on the floor with big smiles and mini-bursts of laughter. The fresh farts slowed with the need to fart.

Liam stood up proud next to King Dollop and his brother. He put his hands on his hips.

Liam inhaled a deep breath and let it out and exclaimed, "The Sweet Smell of Success!" P.J., Liam and Dollop all laughed.

With that, reality started to return to the room. P.J. declared, "Your Majesty, Its time. We really need to get back to our home." The smiles flushed from their face as they realized this was it.

Liam added, "We really need to go make sure Riley doesn't find his way back here…at least for a while." The King glared at him with a temporary concern and then he surveyed the mess in his ballroom. Dollop then said, "Yeah…that's probably a good idea."

"You know where to find us if you ever need us," P.J. sniffed.

"You, too," the King muttered as he hugged them each goodbye.

The two sulking humans dragged their feet as they headed for the broken doorway. P.J. and Liam turned slowly to wave goodbye to the sea of new friends. The Smidgeons all waved back as each one continued cleaning up the mess in front of them.

Liam, with a sudden devilish look in his eye, turned and yelled at the top of his lungs, "Riley!" Hundreds of smidgeons jolted into panic like pinballs, running into each other then bolting for their nearest exits.

Dollop snickered a little under his breath and then shouted, "Stop! He was just kidding!"

Liam held his stomach as he bent over because he was laughing so hard. That was, until he started getting pelted by thrown pieces of nutshell wall, uneaten food off of plates, and finally a handful of Riley-slime in a hard, wet slippery smack across the face. The smile was now off his face and onto the faces of those still throwing "party favors" at him. Liam hunched, trying to cover up as he walked into the tunnel doorway out of sight, yelling back at them all, "Okay, Okay…maybe it wasn't that funny. I guess shouldn't have done that." Dollop slapped his hand on Liam's sticky back and said, "Take care."

King Dollop watched his two new friends-for-life flick pieces of ballroom walls off of themselves. The proud, exhausted king grinned from accomplishment as he watched Liam walk away with a handmade "LICK ME" sign he had stuck to his back. Dollop said to himself, "I hope Riley reads…

Either way, he deserves it."

About the Author

P.M. Kelly brings you this new "larger than life" tale of two brothers. He refined this story while improvising bedtime stories for his sons. The adventure was brought to life from his time with his sons at Cub Scout camp. Kelly was a local scout leader for nearly twenty years and the cover art for *Smidgeons* was illustrated by his Eagle Scout Zach Card.

PM Kelly is a National Literary Classics Top Honors Book Award recipient for his magical fairy tale of a princess in search of dreams, "Dream Butterflies," written for his daughter. Selected from submissions by entrants around the globe, these distinguished honorees are recognized for their contributions to the craft of writing, illustrating, and publishing exceptional literature for a youth audience. In this highly competitive industry these books represent the foremost in literature.

He also invested years volunteering at his local library's children's area and touring other public libraries' children's areas encouraging reading and more. Kelly is a proud father of three inspirational children who lives in a small New England town in the United States.

Made in the USA
Middletown, DE
23 December 2022

17021201R00046